REDEMPTION

S.D. JOHNSON

For my family
and Heidi.
With all my love.

Chapter One

Beth Anderson took the newspaper from her psychiatrist with shaking hands. She fought hard to subdue the panic that rose from the pit of her stomach. It fastened itself in the back of her throat, almost choking her. She had been dreading this moment for weeks.

She read slowly, taking in each detail and trying to preserve the picture of detachment that she presented to the world.

Judge describes rapist as an animal.

Wayne Jackson, 28, of Melbourne Street, pleaded guilty to rape and attempted murder today at Billingham Crown Court.

The judge, Alice Jefferson, described it as an evil and calculated act against a courageous young woman. She said that Jackson had behaved like an animal.

Jackson had been released on license just three days before the offence. He admitted forcing entry into the victim's flat and subjecting her to three hours of torture before raping her and leaving her for dead.

Jackson was caught through DNA traces found by forensic experts at the scene. The judge detained him for psychiatric reports, pending sentencing.

Margaret Astle, the local MP, has called for an enquiry into Jackson's early release. He had been serving a ten-year sentence for aggravated burglary and the rape of a sixty-year-old woman.

She finished reading and then folded the newspaper in half with fastidious precision and laid it down on the coffee table, aligning it exactly with the edge of the table. At least he had had the decency to plead guilty and had saved her from having to give evidence.

This office had always made her feel awkward. It was functional but soulless. It was an office that was used by various professionals during the day, but it belonged to none of them and so no one had tried to leave their mark on it. Even the plastic covered armchairs made both patient and doctor sit up straight, so it was impossible to gain any sense of ease or comfort from the surroundings.

The doctor, a woman in her late thirties, looked like a sensitive, bohemian soul. Her long rust-coloured hair was braided each night and released every morning as a cascade of pre-Raphaelite tendrils. She wore long, flowing skirts, draped gossamer scarves around her neck and glided the corridors noiselessly in her open-toed sandals. Despite this aura of bohemianism, she gave the impression of stifled impatience in her consultations and showed a hint of irritation when she didn't receive her desired responses.

"What are you thinking, Beth?" The doctor spoke after some moments.

"I am thinking that I don't want to talk about it," she said. "In fact, I'd like to leave now."

It was always like this. Beth had resolutely refused to discuss what had happened to her or its paralysing impact. She was willing to talk about the physical injuries and their treatment and progress, but she would not revisit the events of that night when she had woken to find Jackson in her room.

She had answered all the questions that the police had asked, she had complied with everything they had wanted of her. She had undergone every test and examination they had required of her but, when every possible request had been met, she brought down a veil and refused to look back through it.

She had spent several weeks in hospital as her injuries had been extensive and she had also fallen prey to a bacterial infection. This had rendered her delirious for days and had proved resistant to the first batches of antibiotics they had tried.

She had never looked at the infected scars on her chest where he had carved the word "SLAG" in large, ill-formed letters. When they had become infected, she had turned her head away each time they were dressed. She knew the word was there. She had felt every cut of the knife. She knew what it said without anyone telling her. She had watched the movement of his hand and saw the form of each letter as it was created. Talking about it would not remove it, nor would it erase the memory.

The doctor closed the folder and sighed. "If that's what you want, Beth."

"It is,"she replied.

It was easier to say what she didn't want. She didn't want to talk about it with her doctor. She didn't want to attend the group sessions and listen to the pains of others being endlessly rehearsed.

She didn't want to feel vague and unfocussed: the pills left her head in a daze. What had happened had happened. She wanted to put it aside, just as she had put the newspaper aside, and be left alone.

But they wouldn't let her. They looked at the fragile young woman, stuck in her own present, afraid to look forward and terrified to look back and they wanted to release her from this frozen existence.

They wouldn't believe her when she said she needed to be left alone: every day brought attempts to get her to open her heart to them. The scars on her wrists convinced them that she needed their help, that she needed to recover in their prescribed way. They wanted her to talk about what had happened and how she felt and when she wouldn't oblige, they decided she was in denial.

"Where do we go from here, Beth? What do you want to happen?" the doctor asked.

Beth looked at her sadly, shook her head slightly and said, "I haven't decided yet."

The doctor looked past her at the over-sized clock on the opposite wall. Their time allocation had expired so she made a couple of notes in her folder and let Beth leave.

Chapter Two

Beth was not stupid: she knew only too well that they thought she was in denial. The trouble was that she had tried to tell them how she felt, but they dismissed it. She needed someone to listen to her opinion and respect it. She did not want to revisit, analyse or give any importance to what had happened, but their wisdom contradicted every sentence she uttered.

When, at last, she had been discharged from hospital she had returned to her flat. The time she had spent on the hospital ward had allowed her to make detailed plans.

It was hard to face the flat again, with its forensic dust still visible, and everything not quite in its right place. She knew her support officer had done her best to get things put right, but every item that was slightly out of place delivered another stab of mental anguish.

She ordered a supply of cardboard boxes and packing tape on same day delivery and collected a roll of bin bags from the corner shop. She had to pack away all traces of her former life. Every single thing in the small flat was tainted and had to be removed. She booked a collection with a local man with a van. Normally, she would have consigned everything to the charity shop, but she was clear: everything must go to the tip.

She didn't try to fool herself. She was not going to be able to get into her bed that night: it was the bed he'd dragged her from. She knew that, if she was lucky, she might doze on the settee when she felt she could do no more.

She'd bought milk and bread, knowing that a cup of tea and dry toast would be all she could face. She had never, at any time in her life, been so self-aware and so decisive. There was no point buying food that she would simply throw away uneaten. If ever there was a time to be truthful to herself it was then.

She accepted that she was frightened to be in the flat. It was the last place she wished to be, but everything needed to be packed away and sealed to erase that place from her mind so she started straight away by bagging up her clothes.

It was good to be in focus and busy: it kept her in control. The boxes had arrived, and she was able to pack up her possessions. There wasn't that much to do. It was a furnished flat and it came with cooking utensils, crockery and cutlery. It was strangely satisfying to tape up each box and move it on to the growing stack in the hall.

That last night in the flat felt like a relief. The packing was finished and everything would be collected at nine the next morning. She curled up on the settee and gained some satisfaction from knowing that she had removed all traces of herself from the flat.

The van man came ten minutes early: a cheerful, whistling, prematurely aged young man. His clothes reeked of tobacco and his tattoos carried the stories of his life up to that point. The birth dates and names of three children were prominent. He had several teeth missing, but that did not stop him smiling.

"Doing a flit, love?" he asked. "Hope you're up-to-date with your rent." He laughed at his own joke and set to loading his van, whose scrapes and dents told the story of either a reckless driver, or a very unlucky one.

She paid him and closed the door behind him. She had decided not to write to her parents. It would only cause needless guilt because they had no power to delete that night from her memory.

She took a knife from the kitchen, went to the bathroom, climbed in the bath and, with no hesitation, cut her wrists. It was as straightforward, simple and clinical as that.

Chapter Three

Beth was not dead.

It took some time for her to piece together the scene as she gradually came round. She was in the emergency department of the local hospital once more, and there was a frenzy of activity around her. The haze of colours and the blur of voices started to come into focus and she came to a vague awareness of what was happening.

The kind, soothing voices of her previous hospital experiences were absent. Here was front-line life-saving action, delivered by expert staff with almost ruthless efficiency. They were working to save someone who was responsible for her own injuries, and those injuries needed instant and speedy care. She sensed all of this through her emerging sensibility.

Eventually, when the emergency treatment was finished, and her condition was stabilised, they allowed her landlady to come in to see her. She had been the one who had called the ambulance and had stayed, so they assumed there was some connection there.

"So, you pulled through?" she said.

This woman let out the top of her house as a self-contained, furnished flat to supplement her income. It was business, no more than that. She neither befriended her tenants nor involved herself in their affairs. She took infinite pains to screen applicants so that the whole enterprise was as trouble-free as possible. There was no way she could have foreseen or avoided the trouble this girl had brought to her door.

She had seen her property changed into a crime scene. Every inch had been crawled over by forensic scientists and every drawer, wardrobe and cupboard emptied and examined by detectives.

She had had journalists and TV crews on her doorstep, hounding her for interviews or comments. Her property had appeared on the local news and even in the national press.

This was not good for business. She had endured all that without saying a word of protest because she knew the young woman had been through an ordeal. She had suspected that her tenant would move on and had wondered how she was going to market the flat when it had been the scene of a brutal crime.

Things had now got worse. She had seen the van man empty the flat and yet the girl had not given notice. It was true that the rent had been unexpectedly paid in advance for the next three months: she had seen the cash transferred into her account first thing that morning.

She had wanted to know what was going on and, on not getting an answer at the door, she had assumed that the girl had simply left. She didn't blame her, but she did need to know for sure.

She had fetched her master key and let herself in. The girl had been a good tenant: that three months' money bought the time to find a replacement, despite the bad publicity. There was a chance she wouldn't end up out of pocket and, as another positive, the girl had left the flat in spotless condition.

She went from room to room, nodding in satisfaction, until she reached the bathroom.

She thanked God her mobile was in her pocket, she was able to call for an ambulance straight away. The girl did not respond at all to her voice and had been so efficient in emptying the flat that all the towels had been removed. There was nothing there to bind up the wounds.

She was no hero, and she had no sympathy for such selfish behaviour, but she knelt by the bath, took an arm in each hand and applied what pressure she could on both wrists. She wasn't sure if this was the right thing to do but it was all she could think of.

As she waited, she reflected that it was a good job the girl had climbed into the bath. She would soon be able to wash the bath out and at least the mess wasn't on the carpets.

She felt she had to go in the ambulance. She hadn't wanted to, but she was aware how bad it would look if she didn't. The girl was totally unaware she was there and so it was a complete waste of time. It was annoying because the emergency team in A and E took a long time to stabilise her and she'd felt obliged to wait. Now, on top of all that, she faced a two-bus ride journey home and she'd realised she didn't have her bus pass with her.

"Thank you," Beth said. She wasn't sure why her landlady was there or what she had had to do.

"I know you've been through it, but that doesn't entitle you to expect me to be the one to find you and clear up your mess."

"I'm sorry." Her voice was weak.

The woman huffed, as if that apology was woefully inadequate compensation for what she had been through.

"Anyway, you've cleared the flat and paid for your notice, so we'll call it quits. I hope you go on alright." The woman turned and left the bay.

Beth drifted back into the blackness of her oblivion.

Chapter Four

After the emergency treatment was over and she was stabilised they found her a bed in a ward for overnight observation, and then she became a problem.

She was ready for discharge but there was nowhere to discharge her to. She had rendered herself homeless and she was totally without possessions. The only clothes she had left were the blood-stained heap that had been put, soaking wet, into a hospital plastic sack. She had absolutely nothing else.

It was impossible to believe she would not try to end her life again because she had prepared for her demise so meticulously. This had been no cry for help.

She resolutely refused to allow them to contact her parents and, as far as they could discern, she had no support network.

She would not engage with the psychiatric team beyond polite, non-committal replies, nor could she tell them her next intentions. She was not being difficult: she simply did not know the answers herself.

Ultimately, she was blocking a medical bed that was needed and the decision was taken to transfer her to a psychiatric hospital as an in-patient. She hated the idea but could offer no safe alternative that would satisfy them. They moved her quickly: even had they wanted to do more for her, they needed the bed she was occupying.

As they told her of the situation, she could see the inevitability of the move, but it was more a case of wearied resignation than acceptance.

She had awoken from her intended sleep of death to find she had to recreate herself. She was the girl with no past. She had no home, no belongings and absolutely no desire to revisit the events that had brought her to this. She was nobody. Her attempt to escape from it all, so carefully planned, had been foiled by accident and, as she entered the psychiatric unit, she saw no way forward.

The hospital had, in one of its previous incarnations, been the workhouse. It was a tall, forbidding, brick-built fortress-like place. They had tried to make the frontage welcoming, with straggling petunias of every colour overflowing from planters. The lawns and hedges were kept well-trimmed but it remained the place no one went by choice.

The hospital was called The Manor, and its very name was enough to strike dread in the hearts of many. It bore absolutely no resemblance to an inviting English country house. It had been built as an institution and no amount of cheery artwork and friendly posters could disguise the purposed austerity that had been its primary design feature.

The windows were set high in the rooms so that they let in plenty of light but denied the occupants any chance of looking out on the world. The staircases were concrete and seemed to echo with the ghostly footsteps of all who had ever used them. The corridors were tiled, cheerless and seemingly endless. The large dormitories of the workhouse had been subdivided into separate bedrooms, but the furnishings were limited, and the textiles were the regulation NHS easily laundered variety.

The outlook from the dormitories was to the rear of the building and, had Beth stood on her solitary chair, all she would have seen were the former exercise yards, separated by high walls so that, in years gone by, the men and women could not see each other.

Several bathrooms, each equipped with a static shower and a porcelain basin, had been created to serve each floor and there was a separate cluster of utilitarian toilet cubicles.

The common areas, the meeting rooms and the staff offices were largely on the side that overlooked the front. Every attempt had been made to cheer the social areas and dining room but, to Beth, the additions looked like irrelevant splashes of primary colours in an otherwise grey environment.

She was never difficult: she was compliant in most ways. She took her medication; she ate her meals; she kept her small room tidy and she was unfailingly civil to the staff. She just could not talk about her feelings because she deliberately kept her mind empty.

The days blended into one. Beth attended the sessions she was expected to. The group sessions were a trial for her as she had absolutely no intention of sharing her nightmare with a bunch of strangers when she wouldn't allow herself to think of it. She would sit there passively and let her mind drift into its sedated world of blankness, starting suddenly if someone mentioned her name.

She went without complaint to the activity sessions organised by the occupational therapists. These were usually craft-based, with everyone making items that could be sold later at the fund-raising fairs that the friends of the hospital organised. Beth was handy with a needle and so she would sit and sew away at whatever item she was allocated.

She had been there for nearly a month, purposely remaining in her own private bubble, when a visitor asked if she would see him. He was one of the chaplains of the unit and the chaplaincy offered every patient their services: it was up to the patient to decide for themselves whether to accept.

She agreed to see him because she was habitually cooperative. She was quite clear on one issue: she wanted none of his prayers. She knew what it was like to have unanswered prayers. That awful night she had prayed continually: please make him stop; please let someone come; please don't let him do that; please make him go away and, finally, please let him kill me. Every single prayer had gone unanswered and now she had no prayers left and had no wish for anyone else's.

"I'm Matthew Thomas, the chaplain," he said, "and I already know that you're Beth. I'm pleased to meet you."

She looked at him. He was fairly young, possibly in his early thirties, but, in his well-worn tweed jacket and crumpled, over-long trousers, he had a sort of timelessness about him. He was a man at ease with himself and that inner composure was reflected in the comfortable, careless way he dressed. His smile was genuine, it crinkled his whole face, and his manner was relaxed.

"I was told you used to paint so I asked an artist friend of mine if she could find out some materials you might be able to use."

He held out a carrier bag and Beth took it and looked inside. There was a new sketchbook, some used tubes of watercolours, some drawing pencils, a well-used palette and a selection of brushes. She looked at him with suspicion. How could this be a random act of kindness when it was so appropriate?

"I know how time can drag in these places, so I thought you might like to try painting again."

That troubled her. A burst of panic rose in her stomach. The only person who knew she'd ever painted was Josie, the cleaner, who bustled around the day rooms. She had grumbled away to her as she swept the floors about the amount of time her granddaughter was spending on her homework for A Level Art. Beth, in an unguarded moment, had said it had been the same for her. It now seemed that even the cleaners reported back every word. She needed to remember never to say anything worth reporting back.

"We thought watercolours would be the easiest for you to use in here,"

Beth knew at once the underlying health and safety issues she presented. They would never have let her have white spirit or varnishes. He'd dealt with that very neatly and she was grateful for his discretion.

"This is very kind of you. You must thank the artist for me." That was possibly the most she had said in one go since she had been there.

He nodded. Her reaction had been better than he had expected. He had been warned that she was politely detached. He could see the contents of the bag had stirred her interest and that was just the start he wanted. He said that he'd call in again in a week or so and he hoped she would see him.

"Maybe you'll have a painting to show me when I call again," he said.

It felt strange to be have had something close to

a normal conversation, but it felt threatening too. Was he just another person who was there to get her to conform to their expectations? Would he be reporting back to the medics?

She watched him leave the common room knowing that she did not care if she ever saw him again.

He, however, knew that he would definitely be visiting again. He had been moved by her quiet composure despite her distanced presence, and he was convinced the paints had resonated with her in some way. He hoped he could find a way to help her reconnect with the present because her unit senior had admitted the staff were at a loss as to how to get through to her.

He took away with him the image of a haunted young woman who had lost the ability to connect with the present. There was an air of wistful loss about her, as if she did not know quite how to occupy her space in the real world and was living in her private inner world which was void of everything.

Chapter Five

Beth started to paint. Her first two attempts ended up in the bin because she hadn't known what she was trying to achieve: she shed tears of frustration at the results and tore them up. It was strange to cry over stupid paintings, she told herself, when up until that point she had not shed a single tear over what had happened to her.

What could she paint? She had got used to thinking of herself as a girl with no past: a girl who blocked out all memories. As she pondered, she began to realise that she did not want to forget everything. The days up until she moved into town had been happy. She recalled her school days and she saw there was much that she wanted to hold on to. That, however, was for her to know and the staff to guess.

The first successful picture was painted from memory. It was the village shop, where she and her friends went when they got off the school bus. That store had been a treasure house for them: there were sweets and chocolates, of course, but also teen magazines and, best of all, a small cosmetics counter offering a budget range.

Whilst she knew that she would never spend time in front of a mirror applying make-up again, the memory of her friends crowding round the display and trying the samples made her feel warm inside.

The shop was distinctive. It was so old it was probably a listed building, though she wasn't sure. It had white walls, a low, lichen-covered roof and small windows fronted with flower boxes that were full of colour no matter what the season. There had been an ancient delivery cycle chained up outside, with a blackboard advertising the special offers of the day propped against it.

It was so clear in her mind that it was like painting from a photograph. It took a long time: those fine paintbrushes challenged her to add the small detail that the bold acrylic brushstrokes she had used in the past would not have captured. She had painted boldly and confidently at school but now she was painting with meticulous detail, and the concentration it demanded was like an anaesthetic acting on her mind as she worked.

She was busy when Matthew Thomas paid his next, and totally unannounced, visit. She was fully absorbed, unaware of his approach and she started when she sensed him beside her

He was just about to say hello when he saw her painting.

"That's my local shop," he said. He was stunned by the coincidence. "It's directly opposite my parish church."

Had they dragged him in specifically to help her reconnect with her past? Alarm filled her and the dread of conspiracy, the feelings that she had once again been manipulated and that she must trust no one in that place re-emerged.

"Whatever's wrong?" he asked, shocked by her stricken face.

She took minutes to be able to speak, and when she did there was an emotional tremble in her voice.

"Are you really a chaplain here, or have you just been called in to get me talking about my past? Did they get you to give me the paints?"

"I'm truly one of the chaplaincy team and they absolutely didn't give me the paints."

"So, who told you to bring me paints? Who told you to come and talk to me?"

There was panic in her eyes. She saw betrayal everywhere. The change in her alarmed him.

"Josie the cleaner told me you might like them……I was getting under her feet when she was trying to clean the Chaplaincy Office and she said I ought to do something useful, like chatting to you or bringing you some paints, instead of filling in forms. We actually try to touch base with everyone eventually, she just pushed me in your direction."

"I thought she'd told the nurses…" her voice trailed off.

"Very unlikely. She complains that they're so full of themselves they can barely bring themselves to speak to the cleaning staff."

She took a few moments to absorb the information and trust the honesty in his expression before she spoke. "Did you know this is where I grew up?"

"In West Stanton?"

She nodded. "I lived there until about eight years ago, when I moved into town."

It was becoming clear that there was no hidden agenda, just blind chance and therefore, no threat. Her breathing steadied and she began to feel foolish.

He sat down beside her and looked more closely at the painting, aware that she had recorded the scene with an accuracy that surprised him. He used that to restart their conversation, glad to be able to ignore her previous distress in a purposeful way.

"I didn't know that you used to live there. You've really captured the shop. It's still the same, though I believe the bike was stolen long before I moved there."

"How long have you been there?" It was the first time that she had initiated any conversation for weeks.

"Five years. I'll get us coffee, and then I can bring you up to date on the village," he said.

He knew better than to give her a chance to refuse so he stood up immediately. A real break-through, he thought, as he made their coffee. Sometimes, he concluded, his prayers were answered very satisfactorily indeed. He decided against mentioning that to her, and unwittingly avoided throwing a hand grenade into their first minutes of genuine connection.

They chatted over coffee, although Matthew did most of the talking. Beth actually paid attention and responded with a smile and an occasional question as he updated her about the village. He described the way it was changing because of various housing developments and a rapidly expanding population.

By the time he left he had a slightly clearer picture of her real background, not simply the dried-up shell that victimhood had created. He hoped he would get to see the girl she had once been. He could already see her creativity and sensitivity.

He had learned she had left the village for work after sixth form, and soon afterwards her parents had moved abroad. She had trained in accountancy and stayed on at the same firm after she qualified.

He decided not to report back on the conversation they had had that day, even though he felt it was something of a breakthrough. He knew that if any part of it was referred to by the staff, she would see it as a conspiracy. He had seen her panic over the paints.

"I'll tell them we've been talking about your

painting," he said, thinking this might make her mind easier.

"Thank you." She understood the subtext and felt slightly more inclined to see him again, especially since he had now made two visits and had made no offer of prayers or helpful bible passages.

Chapter Six

Matthew was keen to help Beth make progress towards her re-integration into the outside world. He knew she would have stayed in that hospital for ever, sedated and free from any challenge. He despaired of the blankness of her existence, only broken by the few hours she spent painting.

He was told she was still attending group sessions but had continued to decline every opportunity to contribute. She sat on the edge of proceedings, a shadowy presence, not really listening to the outpourings of others. She was there in body, but her mind was absent: absent because she deliberately kept it empty.

He felt he had to do something, or he could see

her remaining in that twilight world for ever. He occasionally reflected on why it was coming to matter so much to him, but it was far more comfortable to concentrate on how he could help.

As other patients started to move towards their discharge they would go out of the hospital for a few hours with their friends or family. He realised this was not possible for Beth. He liaised with her doctor to see if he could take her out of the hospital for an hour or two, as she had no one else. She agreed they should draw up a series of outings, each one a little more demanding than the one before. She insisted that all the outings had to be chaperoned.

Matthew persuaded her to arrange for Josie, the cleaner, to go with them. He explained that she would be a friendly face for Beth and pointed out she was the only person in the hospital who had made any connection with her. The doctor was surprised by his choice, but releasing Josie for a few hours would be easy enough to arrange and would have no impact on the other patients.

Josie was touched that the young priest had asked for her to go. She had worked at The Manor for eight years and this was the first acknowledgment she had received. It came from the one person she really liked and dared grumble at and boss about. Not that she was ever rude to him, she just felt sufficiently relaxed with him to act in her natural, bantering way. She had no idea that he had become fond of her or that he valued her down-to-earth observations about what she saw going on.

Josie was no gossip because she had nothing to gossip about. She knew only what she saw with her own eyes. She was not privy to any sensitive information, but Matthew often thought her common-sense evaluations of what the patients needed came closer to the truth than some of the clinical analyses. She had certainly been correct about Beth and the paints.

Josie had become fond of Beth simply because Beth was polite to her. If she was dusting, Beth would automatically move her things out of the way. If she was vacuuming or mopping Beth would clear the floor of obstructions. She also always said thank you. It wasn't that Beth helped her with the cleaning, it was just that the girl acknowledged her presence and tried to make things easier for her.

Most of the time she felt she was invisible to both staff and patients: their lack of manners was a daily irritation. She thought some of them were downright ignorant, but she liked Matthew. That was why she grumbled at him in her teasing way and allowed herself to mention a patient to him if she thought he could help them.

The plans were made so they went out for a drive first. They didn't stop anywhere, he just drove into the countryside and let Beth get used to being outside the confines of the hospital. Josie chattered away, pointing out this and that and it eased the strangeness of the situation. It changed the dynamic from rehabilitation to recreation and all three were able to relax more than they expected.

Next they went into the village of West Stanton and they had drinks in the deli cafe that had recently opened. They had cakes: Josie chose a Danish pastry, a rare indulgence as she was on a permanent diet, and they chatted happily away.

They went to the cinema one afternoon to see an adventure film and the next week they went to a matinee at the theatre. The three sat in companionable silence during the performance and enjoyed discussing it during the interval and on the journey back to the hospital.

They went to a superstore to allow Beth to get some clothes to supplement her very meagre wardrobe. Josie was familiar with this store and she guided Beth from section to section and offered motherly advice about what would wash well and what wouldn't need ironing. She often despaired of the hospital's perfunctory laundry services and privately thought some of the patients looked like tramps.

On reflection, Matthew and Beth believed that Josie was the real reason behind the success of these small steps at rehabilitation. Beth had not felt like a prisoner out on day release because of Josie's relaxed good nature. It had felt natural to all three of them, as if Josie was a long-standing friend of both of them and they were out and about, just catching up and enjoying each other's company.

These were small steps, pre-approved, chaperoned and well-spaced and Josie watched with satisfaction as Beth readjusted steadily. Some sense of real life had come back into the blankness of the girl's world and she had learned to smile occasionally once again.

Josie kept Matthew up to date on the subtle changes she saw in Beth day-to-day. She had played her part to perfection and neither of them ever realised that her stream of chatter had been a well-constructed device to take away the awkwardness that damaged young woman felt as she left the safety of the institution for the first few times.

Josie had the knack of getting Beth to say what she was really thinking, and, on their outings, two things emerged. Beth did not have the will or the courage to return to her old stressful career: the pace of life in the town would be overwhelming. She did not have the confidence to try to re-establish herself in somewhere new. Josie saw that the young woman's mind was in action at last, and that pleased her.

These realisations helped Beth conclude that a move back to West Stanton might allow her to eventually leave the hospital. When she had these thoughts sufficiently clear in her mind, she discussed them with Matthew Thomas. By that time she trusted him enough to speak openly.

He too had been thinking that a return to the village might work for her, but he saw it was important to her to make her own decisions. His job would be to try to help her with her plans, not make them for her. It was a relief when Beth brought the subject up, although he knew it would be a while before she would be ready to leave.

"I want them to ease me off the drugs," she said. "I need to feel ups and downs again. This flat line existence makes me feel like a robot. It isn't real. I need to know if I can be myself again and cope with real life. I can't trust myself to cope out of here whilst I feel so…so…sedated." She couldn't access the word she really needed to describe her detached state of awareness.

He thought she'd expressed herself with remarkable clarity, "I think that would be the first step towards making your plans happen. You need to speak to your doctor and explain again exactly how you feel."

She nodded, aware that he was right, but this time she'd have to do it more forcefully. She had to make her understand. Every previous attempt had failed miserably. The doctor seemed to listen to only what she wanted to hear.

"In the meantime, could you start to think about how I might get back to the village? I'd need somewhere to stay." She smiled ruefully, "I still have some money. I shredded all of my bank statements and cut up the cards, but the accounts are open. I could manage for a while before I can find some work."

"Work?"

"If I can," she said.

It was good for Matthew to know that Beth was getting ready to face life again and he wanted to support her wish to come off the drugs. He felt she was being realistic, and he certainly thought he might be able to help her find somewhere to live. He had a number of caring and supportive parishioners.

He knew he would have to talk all this over with the doctor. When she invited him to sit at her table when he was struggling to find a seat in the cafeteria, he took the opportunity.

He started the conversation by going over Beth's outline plans. He voiced his opinion that they seemed completely viable and that he was happy to support her

"I've been meaning to have a word," her doctor said. "You seem to have become very friendly with each other, and you seem to be prepared to go to an awful lot of trouble for her. Now it looks as if you could be involved in her move away from here. Be aware that I don't think she could cope with any complications right now."

Matthew put down his cup with sufficient force to slop the contents over its rim.

"I've talked every step through with you. I've had your agreement for everything we've done together: in fact, you helped me plan them. You've known me long enough that your so-called complications should never have crossed your mind!"

"Just as long as you remember where the boundary lies," she said.

"Good God, the girl's completely traumatised. Do you really think I'd be lusting after her?"

"Of course not, but you might find yourself becoming fond of her, if you're not already." She had not expected his reaction to be so strong.

It had been a very awkward and strained conversation, and both were glad to finish their coffee and part. Matthew went straight to his car, needing to get away and feeling unclear about where his excessively strong reaction had come from.

He kicked the front tyre in frustration. He was surprised by the strength of his reaction, but the release of stress felt good, so he kicked it once more, even harder. As he got into the car, he saw the doctor at the window, watching him. He wished she had not been looking and he wondered what she made of his tantrum.

Chapter Seven

The steady reduction of the drugs was a lengthy process, but the decreases were so slight that there were no problematic withdrawal symptoms. Little by little, Beth started to feel more connected to the world around her and increasingly aware that she needed to leave.

Her life seemed so regulated and unchallenging that she began to feel stifled. She was still resisting the pressure to share her experience and her feelings and now that she was less sedated this brought a tension into her existence that she did not need.

Beth felt the panic rising as Matthew was eventually able to outline the progress he had made for her return to the village. He had been so kind, so supportive and now it seemed imminent and not quite as straightforward as she had imagined.

"I've asked Laura Dale, one of our deacons, to let you stay with her. She lives on her own with her dog. She's absolutely brilliant. She works none-stop for the parish," he said.

She thought about what he had said. This Laura Dale seemed a little too much involved in the church.

"Matthew, I want to get back to the village," she said, "but I won't be going to your church. She might not approve of that and not want me to stay."

He looked a little startled. He had assumed that she would be happy to lodge with a good-hearted single woman. "You can change your mind about helping me if you like. I wouldn't blame you."

"Help me to understand," he said, "because I won't be changing my mind."

She paused, getting her thoughts into order. It was the closest she had come to communicating her real inner turmoil to any person, even herself.

He waited. He started to move to put his hand on hers but changed the move into a simple shift of position. The doctor's words were still stinging, and he was trying to ensure that every word, every gesture was totally appropriate.

She sighed from the bottom of her soul. "That night, the night it happened, I prayed harder than I've ever done. I prayed over and over again for him to go. What makes me so mad is not just that my prayers weren't answered, it's the church's belief that all that man has to do is say he's sorry and he's all forgiven, washed as white as snow."

He nodded gravely. Forgiveness was one of his core beliefs and now he could see exactly where her anger was coming from.

"He only has to say two words, I'm sorry, and that's it. It's all over for him, total peace of mind and complete forgiveness. But I don't forgive him, and what magic two words do I say, Matthew, to make it be all over for me?"

She paused to find the right words and then she carried on. "If I understand it all correctly, I have to forgive him. He says sorry and that's it. I have to forgive him for bludgeoning me with a hammer, raping me, sodomising me, carving slag on my chest and leaving me for dead. That's all. Just forgive him. Well, I can't, and if I don't forgive him, I'm the sinner."

He was stunned at the way she had finally put

her ordeal in words: he had had no idea of the extent of the attack until then and it was worse than he had imagined. It amazed him to discover that what tortured her the most was the ease with which Jackson could gain absolution compared to the horror and hatred she had to carry with her endlessly. He had never heard such a reasoned challenge to the beliefs he had cherished for so long and were the pillars of his ministry.

He had no answer, no response, at that moment to ease her pain because he could think of no theological doctrine adequate to reassure her or quell her anger.

"I could just say you must put your trust in God, but, from where you're standing, that must be the last thing you want to hear."

She nodded. "I don't mean to be rude but I need your practical help, not your sermons."

"Then there will be no sermons but plenty of help. I can find you somewhere else to stay," he said, suddenly feeling totally inadequate.

"Or you can make your deacon understand that I'm just wanting temporary lodgings, not salvation," she shook her head. "I don't want to make it hard for you when you've got me a place to live, but this really matters."

"Laura will understand," he said, demonstrating his weakest flaw. He believed in people and how they appeared to him. He did not question motive and he did not look for hidden agenda: he looked for the good in people and usually found something to value.

Laura Dale, the deacon, was not impressed when she next saw Matthew and heard the terms Beth had laid down. She understood that this girl had experienced some sort of trauma and that she had been in a psychiatric hospital, but she was a woman who knew no self-doubt. She had no time for people who could not stand up to a bit of adversity. She wasn't sure she really wanted this weak girl weeping and wailing around her house, although Matthew had assured her that she was perfectly composed.

She was also annoyed by the care that he seemed to be prepared to lavish on this girl. It seemed disproportionate when she thought about all of his other responsibilities. She was even preparing for ordination herself so that she could take some more of the strain off him. Now he wanted her to accept that the girl who would be staying with her was not remotely interested in the church and she wasn't to even try to encourage her.

The way he treated her annoyed her at times. He always knew where she was when he wanted help, but she was beginning to think those were the only times he thought of her.

She had tried to win him over through her good deeds. She didn't emphasise her femininity in any way. Her clothes were practical, she cut her own hair in a chunky, choppy fashion and she did not own a single piece of make-up. Her only concession to cosmetics was a can of heavy-duty anti-perspirant. She had sufficient self-awareness to know that she had a problem.

She wasn't to know he saw her as a good soul, a willing servant of the church and an immensely strong and practical person who would make Beth feel safe whilst she stayed in her home. She would have been mortified if she'd known he thought she looked like the sort of woman who could stand up for herself and Beth in the event of trouble. He also thought that her dog, the rescued Labrador-cross, Samson, would be good company for Beth when she was alone in the house.

Laura, always seeking to please, appeared to

agree with him whole-heartedly on what would be best for Beth and promised through gritted teeth that she would provide shelter, but not offer salvation.

She got a room ready for Beth in the small terraced house that she had inherited from her aunt with resentment already surfacing in her heart, aware that she had to keep it hidden from Matthew.

Beth had listened carefully to Matthew's description of her landlady and imagined her to be a brisk, capable woman, but caring beneath a tough exterior. She had had no misgivings in accepting, having been assured that Laura Dale knew her soul was not there for saving.

Chapter Eight

Matthew admitted to himself privately that he was at a loss for the first time since he had found his vocation. Beth's words had gone deep and challenged him to the core of his beliefs. He found her arguments compelling when he considered them from her perspective, and he had not found a convincing response.

He was also troubled by his own motivation. Was he simply doing his pastoral duty, or was his concern for her more personal? He ended up doing what he always did in crises. He read his bible with renewed fervour. He prayed in the solitude of the empty church, allowing its silence and sanctity to engulf him and bring focus into his words.

He did his duties diligently. He presented his friendly, caring demeanour to the world so that everyone assumed that his mind was untroubled. He tried to be the tower of strength and rock of unwavering certainty that they expected.

Matthew Thomas conducted services, preached his sermons, visited the sick, comforted the bereaved and laid the dead to rest. He maintained his chaplaincy work, went to his meetings, chaired the church council, drank tea with the Mothers Union members and threw his energies into his favourite project.

The questions Beth had posed gnawed at him constantly and he kept himself busy as he wrestled with the challenge to his previously unwavering certainties.

He worked tirelessly whenever he could at the centre for the homeless and vulnerable on the edge of town that had been set up by the diocese. It was not a particularly popular enterprise with his parishioners because it took him away from them so much. It was where he saw real need and, now that his mind was troubled, where that he found his sense of purpose. Each time he visited, he knew that this was where he really wanted to be. The cosy comfort of the parish was not feeding his soul or easing his mind.

He had supported Beth as she moved into the village. It was not proving as easy as he expected or hoped. He had tried dropping in at Laura Dale's to see Beth in the first few days, but Laura always took these visits over. There was always some essay she wanted him to look over or a parishioner she needed to discuss. He was surprised by her lack of tact and sensitivity towards her house guest.

"You don't mind if we pop into the other room, do you Beth? There's something I really need to discuss with Matthew," Laura would say, and, just as Beth could hardly object, so Matthew could hardly refuse.

In the end, he made an arrangement to catch up with Beth when she walked Samson, and, from that first meeting, they fell into a routine that Laura Dale was unaware of.

Beth could see from the beginning that Laura resented her and that she'd only taken her in to help Matthew. She also knew that he was totally oblivious to all of this. She decided discretion was the safest course, though she did feel sorry for Laura having to share her home with someone she clearly didn't like.

She also felt a little bit guilty that Samson had become her greatest fan. If she sat in the living room in the evening when Laura was there, he would curl at her side and rest his heavy head on her feet.

When she first slept there, he would follow her upstairs and whimper softly at her door. Beth and Samson eventually reached an understanding. She would open her door, as quietly as she could, a few minutes after she heard Laura switch her light off. He would pad in and heave his heavy body on to the end of her bed. As soon as he heard Laura stirring in the morning, he would struggle off the bed and go and compose himself into a picture of dedication and wait for her to open her door.

Beth knew that the down-to-earth Laura would disapprove of dogs in the bedroom but having Samson on the foot of her bed brought her the sense of security she needed to allow herself to go into a deep sleep. She was sleeping properly without the aid of drugs for the first time since her nightmare began and it felt good.

One day she told Matthew about this as they walked Samson and they laughed together in admiration of the dog's intelligence rather than at his deception of Laura. They never discussed Laura, although both were aware they had a common understanding that things were far from ideal.

"Do you feel ready to do some work?" he asked as they sat together on the seat at the edge of the park.

"To be honest, I'd be glad to do something. I'm actually finding myself getting bored now that I'm not drugged out of my mind. What do you have in mind?"

"Marie at the deli-cafe was telling me that she can't get to grips with the bookkeeping and her tax returns and I thought you could give her a hand. She's happy with the baking and the shop side, but she's got no head for figures and she's at the point where she's looking for an accountant."

Beth thought this over and could see it might be just the opportunity she needed. Perhaps, starting from there she could take on a few more clients and build up a small business just working from home. She knew she needed an income before she could look for a place of her own, and she knew she had to do that quickly.

She felt reassured as they talked it through. He said he would fix up a meeting between the two of them so they could sort something out. He was aware it had been an enormous undertaking for her to move out of the hospital and relocate in the village. He was becoming concerned that the lodging arrangements were not really working out so he was glad she felt strong enough to consider meeting Marie and getting back to work. That could lead to her moving out of Laura's.

Beth was pleased to have the opportunity to work again and have the means to find somewhere else to live. She was certainly feeling much better now and was becoming more upbeat and positive She was sure that Samson's devotion had had a positive effect on her mood and outlook.

Financially, she knew she was only coping by dipping into her savings and they were running low, so she did need to start earning again and this seemed an ideal opportunity to make a start. The deli-cafe was a relatively new business and she thought she would be able to get things sorted reasonably easily.

It felt good to have the chance to put her old skills to use without the intensity of working in a busy office. She didn't want to be working to tight deadlines or dealing with the stress she had once accepted as normal.

Chapter Nine

It was a quiet day in the cafe when Beth called in to talk about the bookkeeping. She liked Marie straight away: she was a friendly, enthusiastic woman with a cheerful smile.

They bonded immediately and Marie suggested that Beth should work on the books in the small office in the back of the cafe. It was fully equipped with a pristine computer and printer and Marie had bought a professional accounting package that she had not even managed to install. Marie knew that she needed help urgently and Beth offered extremely reasonable rates.

Marie knew from Matthew that Beth was recently discharged from The Manor. She had had her share of experience of mental illness and was totally supportive about Beth's situation. She knew better than to ask questions, but she could recognise someone doing their best to rebuild a shattered life and she respected her courage.

It was the start of a happy working relationship and, over the weeks, Marie introduced several friends to Beth who were running small businesses and were glad to have accountancy services that they could actually afford.

Marie was happy for her to do all this work from her office in return for a substantial discount on her fees. This prevented Beth from having to ask Laura's permission to work from her house and use her computer and wifi. Beth's laptop had been consigned to the tip with all her other things.

It meant she could instil some structure and routine into her life and that helped her feel she was making real progress. She didn't have nearly enough business to keep her occupied full time, so she went into the office late morning each day and stayed until around three thirty. She always walked Samson before starting work.

Marie provided welcome company. They would have a coffee and sit and chat after the lunch time rush was over. It was a welcome taste of normality for Beth. She was beginning to relax enough to talk without feeling panic welling up inside her or worrying that she wouldn't think of anything to say. Marie made conversation seem easy.

She was also confident enough to be totally honest to Marie about the health of her business at this early stage of its existence as the picture emerged from the figures. The updated books told their own story: the income from the catering services for private functions and events was keeping the business afloat. She was particularly reliant on a substantial source of income from the wife of the local MP.

Tess Hargreaves was using Marie to cater for all of her charity events and committee meetings and her cronies, as Marie called them, had also started to use her services. It was clear that, at that point, Tess Hargreaves' custom and her connections were absolutely vital to Marie's survival. The cafe-deli was not yet generating enough income to keep her business going and the only way she could afford to meet her overheads was to keep accepting as many of the outside jobs that Tess Hargreaves put her way.

It was not the news that Marie had hoped to hear, but it confirmed what she already suspected. It meant that she had to stay in Tess Hargreaves' good books and that was not the easiest thing to accomplish because the woman was hyper-critical and demanding.

It was during this conversation that Beth agreed to provide Marie with a hand on an ad-hoc basis. She would help out preparing the food for the larger outside catering jobs that Marie took on. Being able to say yes, without any hesitation, to taking something else on made her realise what a distance she had travelled since those days of blankness in The Manor.

Beth was working in the office one afternoon when Tess Hargreaves arrived. Beth always knew when Tess was in the cafe because she had one of those ringing, cut-glass voices that echoed through walls. She couldn't make out what was being said, but she was aware Tess was holding court.

She was in a tremendous flap that day and wanted Marie's help. Her nanny had walked out on her just an hour before and had left her in the lurch. She had left her two children, Martha and Henry, with the cleaner for a while and had come out for coffee to try to calm down and ask if Marie could offer a solution.

"I have to be in London at the weekend," she explained. "I cannot tell you how important it is, and the cleaner would never step in for that long."

Tess Hargreaves was in her early thirties and was always extremely well-groomed and immaculately and expensively dressed. Following Beth's financial revelations Marie had made a point of sitting with her when she called in on her own and always asked about her family. She supplied endless lattes free of charge, as if she were entertaining a friend. Beth doubted Marie would ever have chosen to keep her company in this way if not for her financial situation. As things stood, she made sure she was always available with a smile and a sympathetic ear.

Marie was suitably sympathetic but could offer no solution. She knew of no one available for childcare. She went back to the counter whilst Tess made a few phone calls but when she returned Tess had drawn a blank with each one. Tess was especially annoyed that the agency she used regularly was unable to help. She was becoming increasingly desperate.

At that moment Beth had to interrupt to ask

Marie to take a phone call in the office. Tess's eyes zoned in on her like a missile. She had occasionally seen Beth in the cafe over the last few weeks but had not taken much notice of her before but, looking at her that day, she looked calm and capable, clean and tidy and very responsible.

When Marie had finished the call and returned to the table Tess was ready with her questions. "Does that girl work for you at the weekend?"

Marie was amazed that Tess had latched on to Beth as a possible solution. The woman didn't even know her.

"Do you think she'd be any good at looking after children?"

"She's an accountant by profession. She took over my book keeping a few weeks ago," Marie replied, thinking that would be sufficient to repel Tess's interest. Accountants were not known for seeking childcare jobs.

"But she's not here at the weekend?" Tess continued.

Marie was astonished that Tess was still pursuing the possibility of Beth caring for her children.

"No, but I doubt she'd want to," Marie said. "I believe she's been quite ill and is only just recovering." She dare not say more for fear of betraying Beth's confidence, although she was sure if Tess knew how recently Beth had been discharged from The Manor the matter would have been closed.

"I can only ask," Tess said, undeterred. "You have no idea how important it is. You did know that Oliver's been made a junior minister at the Treasury?"

Marie nodded; she had seen it in the newspapers. She took it that this promotion necessitated Tess being in London to support him in some official event, but Tess did not confirm.

"I will ask her," Tess said, emphasising the word "will". "She can only say no. Could you ask her to come over?"

Marie was truly astonished that this wealthy woman really intended to ask a complete stranger to look after her two children over the weekend. She could appreciate her need to support her husband, but this was beyond belief.

Marie was horrified and she was thinking rapidly. At first she was tempted to refuse but two factors changed her mind: she knew Beth would be totally capable of making up her own mind, despite her recent troubles, and she knew that she risked losing Tess's business if she crossed her on this. She decided to leave it entirely up to Beth and then Tess could not blame her if she said no.

Marie popped into the office and very quickly briefed Beth on what she was going to be asked. Beth was flabbergasted.

They walked back to the table together. "Have you met Mrs. Hargreaves?" Marie enquired.

"No," Beth said, smiling at her uncertainly, "though I've seen you in the cafe, of course."

Tess Hargreaves nodded in her direction and pulled out a chair and patted the seat.

"I thought you might be able to help," Tess explained. "My nanny just walked out on us this morning and it has left me in a total mess."

Beth wondered why the nanny had walked out but was too polite to ask.

"My cleaner is caring for the children at the moment, but she can't help beyond that. I'm literally desperate to find someone. You know my husband is a junior minister now? I have to be in London at the weekend and I simply cannot take them with me. I was hoping, praying in fact, that you might be able to help?"

Beth was totally amazed that a total stranger would ask her to do this. It made no sense to trust someone she didn't know with her children. As was her custom, Beth paused to reflect before replying.

"I don't know anything about taking care of children," she said honestly. "I'm really not the right person."

"Martha is four and Henry is three," Tess Hargreaves continued, as if Beth had not spoken. "They are adorable," she said, "and they are no trouble, no trouble at all. You need to come to meet them," she continued. "Obviously, we're talking about just the weekend, but the full-time job comes with accommodation, a car, all meals and a good salary. My husband spares no expense where the children are concerned."

"I really don't know what else to say. I'm glad you would ask me, but I actually don't feel equipped." Beth had no experience whatsoever of young children and was just getting used to being in charge of her own life. She didn't feel she was in a position to take responsibility for two more.

"Then come and see how things are and meet Martha and Henry," Tess said. "I'm sure you'll want to help when you meet them. I'll expect you at ten in the morning." With that, she stood, shook her lustrous hair back over her shoulders and picked up her Bayswater bag, swinging it emphatically over her arm. She nodded her farewell and left.

Beth looked in astonishment at Marie. "Did that just happen? I feel shell-shocked."

"She was a lot more forceful than I expected. I thought we were just going to chat about the possibility," Marie said apologetically. "What ever will you do?"

Beth sighed and stood up, "I'll sleep on it," she said. "I can always telephone her in the morning. Her number's in the office files."

She knew what she would do to gain focus because Tess had put her in such an impossible situation. She would talk it through with Matthew Thomas and, until she'd done that, she wouldn't even consider going to meet the children.

She went directly from the cafe and over to the church hoping he would be there. The door was open, and she slipped in silently and took a seat just inside. Matthew had finished a meeting with some new parents seeking a baptism for their baby and was sitting on the front pew, head bowed. She was glad to see there was no one else there and waited patiently until he crossed himself, stood up and walked down the aisle.

He beamed when he noticed her. This was the first time she had ever stepped foot into the church since her return to the village.

"Beth," he said, "how lovely to see you."

She stood up uncertainly. "I was wondering if we could have a chat about something."

"Of course," he said. "Come through to the vestry."

"Somewhere neutral?" she asked.

He shrugged, there had, after all, been no change in her attitude. "How about the pub? It's only just opened so it will be quiet."

He collected his jacket and secured the church, and then walked with her across the road to the Boar's Head. She hadn't been in there since her return to the village, but it had hardly changed. The bench seating around the edge of the lounge was still covered in the dingy dark brown PVC, with black sticky tape covering the gashes it had suffered over the years.

The tables were just the same, with their heavy wooden tops and black cast iron bases. The old wheel-back chairs were tucked in beneath them. It was as if time had stood still.

They took a table in the corner and Matthew went to fetch their drinks.

She told him of Tess Hargreaves' request and asked him what he thought. It took him some time to reflect before, as his answer, he asked her what she thought.

"That's unfair," she said. "I asked you that."

"I think it's outrageous of her to ask," he said, unusually frank. "She hasn't a clue who you are."

Beth nodded. "I really don't know anything about children," she said, "but I do know they'd be safe with me over the weekend. I'm scared she's so desperate she might ask someone......"

She searched for the right word. "Unsuitable," she added at last. It was the best she could think of.

"But that's not down to you. It's not your responsibility. What did Marie say?" he asked.

"The same as you. That she was being irresponsible," Beth said, "which she is. I'm just worried about those children."

"Which their mother is clearly not. Anyway, before you think about this you need to ask yourself if you are well enough," he said. "Could you be alone overnight with them? There would be no Samson."

"That's what I'm not sure about."

They lapsed into silence, both aware that the situation they were discussing was completely ridiculous and that Tess Hargreaves had had no right to ask her in the first place. They both sensed that Beth was already starting to feel some responsibility towards the children.

"If she left them with someone else and anything happened, I'd feel responsible," she admitted.

"Without any reason," he said. "Her irresponsibility isn't a reason for you to step in."

"It's starting to feel that it is," Beth said, and Matthew did not feel easy about her getting involved.

Chapter Ten

Before she left the café, Beth checked with Marie where the Hargreaves lived. Marie had no idea of the bombshell she was about to drop when she replied that they lived in a house called The Willows, just behind the church.

The Willows. That had been her home when she had lived in the village. She knew her parents had rented it out since they moved abroad, but she had never interested herself in the details.

She wasn't sure what she felt about the possibility of spending the weekend in her former home, but she was so accustomed to keeping her own counsel that Marie suspected nothing.

Tess Hargreaves opened the door and showed her into the sitting room. Her parents' furniture, with its ageless style, was still in place. They had obviously let their home furnished, but, with the Hargreaves' accessories and photographs and Tess's obvious skill at dressing a room, it looked like it belonged only to her.

The two children were sitting in front of the giant television, engrossed in their program. Tess called them over. "Martha, Henry, come and say hello to Beth. She will be coming to look after you this weekend".

That was awkward, Beth thought to herself. Matthew had been absolutely correct when he'd warned her that Tess approached negotiation like a bulldozer. The children looked at her with slightly increased interest. They came over at once, eyes still lingering on the TV screen.

"Hello you two," Beth said.

They smiled shyly and the little girl, the elder, said hello.

"Tell me what you usually do," Beth said.

"We have breakfast in the kitchen," Martha said confidently. "We have cornflakes and toast. Then we go to the nursery to watch TV. We go to bed after lunch for our nap and then we get up and do our drawing. After tea we have our baths and go to bed."

"Do you do that every day?" Beth asked.

"Every day, except swimming day," Martha replied.

Tess beamed. Her daughter was very articulate for her four years. "I told you they are no trouble," she said.

Beth was aghast at the limitations of their daily routine, and astonished to see that their mother approved.

"Can you show me your nursery please, Martha? I'd really love to see it." She turned to Tess to see if she agreed, and she nodded.

Martha obviously blossomed with responsibility and led the way up the two flights of stairs to the large attic area. This had once held her father's studio for his architectural design business and his huge drawing board used to dominate the largest room. The walls had been covered with his drawings and plans and it seemed strange without them.

Everything had changed. Her father's large studio, his office, his meeting room and cloakroom had all been recommissioned. The large room was now the nursery playroom. She was staggered by the wealth of toys, books and games that were neatly stacked in the modern storage units the Hargreaves had installed. The room was no longer dominated by the old drawing board but by an enormous wall-mounted television.

There were now two bedrooms. One for the children and the other for the nanny. The children's room was charming, with skilful murals on the otherwise blank walls. The nanny's room was furnished in the style of a budget hotel, with fitted furniture and neutral drapes. There were tea and coffee items and a kettle alongside the wall-mounted TV. The old cloakroom was now a bathroom.

Beth took in all the details without appearing to stare. She could see at a glance that the top floor was perfectly equipped for childcare, yet the toys lay mostly unused. Their young lives had, to that point, she believed, been soulless and regimented.

She started to get the strangest and most disturbing feeling that she was needed there, and it took her by surprise. She had been so focussed on getting her life on track she hadn't had anyone else to think about, and now the thought of those little children with their empty eyes was gnawing away at her.

"You've got a lovely nursery," she said, smiling at the children. "You do keep it nice and tidy," she said.

"Mummy likes it to look nice," Martha said gravely, "and so we keep everything in its place. We don't really get much out."

Tess Hargreaves could not have been more pleased with her two children. She was convinced that they were creating the right impression on Beth. She had no idea that Beth was feeling sorry for them and that was why she was beginning to think she should look after them that weekend.

It was strange but Beth was already thinking of how to give the two children some fun. That was ironic. There had been no fun in her life for as long as she could remember, but, in her heart, she felt desperately sorry for them. She was beginning to think she could provide something more stimulating than their daily television viewing.

"Could I see the kitchen? Is there food in for the weekend?"

"Of course," Tess said, starting to feel a tiny bit triumphant that once again she was going to have her own way. "The freezer is absolutely full."

They went down to the kitchen. It was just as she remembered it, but now it was pristine. It had always been their family room, at the centre of life in the old days, but now it looked as if the family only passed through it occasionally.

Reassuringly, the old table where she had sat to do her homework was still in the centre of the room, its familiar old dents and scratches still visible. A good place for painting and craft, she thought, just like it used to be.

"Go and watch the television," Tess said to the children. "I need to talk to Beth."

They went off back to the sitting room quite happily. Tess went on to outline what she needed Beth to do whilst she was away.

"Thank you for letting me see the children," Beth said after all the details had been given. "You need to know that I've been ill lately, and I had to spend some time in The Manor before I started to work for Marie. I understand that you may not want me to look after your children."

Local people all knew that The Manor was a residential psychiatric hospital and it was part of the local vernacular to say "I'll end up in The Manor" when things were stressful or when they'd made a silly mistake. For all the impact her words had on Tess, Beth might as well have said that she had just been on a cruise.

"Marie says you're wonderful, and she said the vicar recommends you." Tess seemed disinterested in the fact that the woman she was leaving her children with had had a recent mental illness, and, for all she knew, might still be suffering from it.

"So, are you going to help me?" she asked. "When would you come over?"

"I'll let you know within the hour," she said. "If I come, I would need to bring some things over on Friday, after work."

"You may as well stay over on Friday and then you'll be here ready on Saturday. I need to get away early." Tess was still not registering the possibility of a refusal.

She was actually surprised that Beth needed time to think because she had been convinced she had won her over. She imagined the girl would have leapt at the chance to make a lot of money so easily and stay in such a lovely house with such compliant children.

She led Beth through to say goodbye to the children and gave her her card in readiness for the call to her mobile. The children were sitting cross-legged on the floor, eyes glued to CBeebies, but they responded immediately to their mother and said goodbye to Beth politely.

Chapter Eleven

Beth's mind was frenzied as she walked back to the café and she was exceedingly surprised that there was a tremor of excitement in the pit of her stomach.

She had had little to do with small children, she had nothing but her common sense to rely on about their care, but everything told her that those children needed her, even if it was just for a couple of days.

She had never seen such underprivileged, privileged children in her life and the oxymoron fascinated her. There was an emptiness in their eyes, a total lack of spark and, despite all her inexperience she was sure she could look after them better than their previous nannies and introduce some interest to their limited little lives. She realised she could be totally misjudging their situation, but she didn't think she was.

On the downside, she disliked the thought of being alone with the children when both parents were away. She knew her parents had had an ancient alarm in the house, but they had given up on it long before they left. She needed to check if there was an efficient security system. She imagined that there would be because of Oliver Hargreaves' position, but she would need to check. She would be of no use to the children if she was scared out of her wits to be alone with them in the house, and she could hardly kidnap Samson and take him with her.

"How did you get on?" Marie asked.

Beth was far too guarded by habit to react any other than cautiously. "I'm just making sure. I'm going to get back to her." She went to the office and back to her bookkeeping.

She re-emerged after about half an hour to join Marie for coffee.

"It is so good to have something to think about," she said. "My mind is swimming with activities we can do. We can try baking; we can try craftwork. Oh, Marie, it feels so right."

"Here's to you, Mary Poppins," she said, raising

her coffee cup. "You've obviously decided to do it. I'll be on the end of the phone if you need help. You can't really lose, it's only for a weekend: it's not as though you're signing up for life."

She chinked coffee cups with Marie and smiled. "If only I could take Laura's Samson with me," she said.

"I think Samson might agree with you on that," Marie observed.

Beth called Tess and agreed to look after the children.

Chapter Twelve

There were a number of things Beth wanted to clarify when she called round later that afternoon. The security of the house when she was alone with the children was her greatest anxiety.

She was relieved that there was now a state-of-the-art security system installed, with a direct link to the police station. It had not occurred to her before but, when Tess explained, it was obvious that an M.P. and junior minister, and one with as high a profile as Tess's husband, would be provided with a sophisticated security system.

"And there's always Boo,' Tess said with a laugh. "That's the dopey labradoodle that Oliver bought for the children and, of course, he had to call it

Boudica. The last nanny couldn't stand it in the house so now it resides in the outhouse with its own run. The Dogman takes it for a few hours each day and cleans up after it, so as long as you feed it, it will be fine."

The Dogman was the local dog-walker, everyone called him that, and Beth vaguely remembered him from her youth. She filed a mental note. Boo could be incorporated into night-time security that weekend.

She had a check list that she needed to work through. It was largely the common-sense things that had popped into her brain, that had been hyperactive since she had said she'd look after the children.

The children had no medical conditions to worry about, they had no medication to take but could have Calpol if they developed a temperature, they were not enrolled in any classes that weekend, they were patients at the local medical centre but, being weekend, Tess provided the emergency number.

Tess was impressed by the list of things that Beth wanted to know and that seemed to her to confirm that she was an excellent judge of character and the children would be well cared for. She considered she had handled the whole childcare issue with skill, and she was able to wave Beth off with a fair degree of smugness.

Laura greeted the news that Beth would be spending the weekend away with barely disguised glee. She had come to resent the girl's apparent hold over Matthew Thomas, which she considered to be unfair, considering all she did for the parish.

She had worked so hard on his behalf and all she could gather from him was that he thought she was an absolute star, whatever that meant. She knew he thought he could always rely on her for help. He had certainly got that wrong: it had never been her intention to become a lackey, not even for him. Having Beth to stay had pushed her to the edge.

She would also be glad not to witness her own dog fawning over Beth, even if just for a couple of days. She didn't know how she'd kept her bedroom door closed firmly shut when she heard him plod up the stairs to join Beth each night. She wanted to command him to go downstairs but she never did, vaguely aware the silly girl was nervous about night time security.

Beth had learned to be adept at role play in The Manor, and the quiet, unfailingly polite, private, insulated, isolated, self-contained character she had retreated into there was the person who had lived with Laura. It was that person who took her temporary leave that Friday evening.

Matthew was driving her and her bag of belongings round to The Willows. This annoyed Laura because that was one of his nights at the centre and it was selfish of Beth to make him run the risk of being late. She was only going to be away for the weekend and the bag was small and light. She could have walked over quite easily.

She had, of course, offered to drive her over but Matthew had insisted it was no trouble to him. Beth was relieved because she really didn't want Laura nosing around The Willows' nursery and her room.

Tess kept the children with her whilst Beth moved her few things in and then she brought them upstairs to put them to bed. It was strange, when

Beth came to look back on those few days, this would be the one helpful and unselfish thing that she would ever remember Tess doing.

That evening, Beth curled up on the settee in the room she knew so well and tried to read. She didn't care much about TV, and she didn't want its sound to disturb the children. She looked in on them before she went to bed and felt strangely moved at the sight of them, so tiny in their beds, hugging their soft toys tightly.

It felt strange but oddly right to settle into bed that night. She heard the beeping of the alarm as it set, and her anxieties eased. She could hear the familiar ticking of the grandfather clock in the hall and it reminded her of all those childhood nights when she had listened to its resonant sound. She had noticed that the Hargreaves had silenced the strike and she knew she would miss its familiar chimes.

She pulled the duvet around her ears and went to sleep almost straight away. It was as if she was at last somewhere she felt she belonged.

She was woken by a shrill scream at around two o'clock. She ran barefoot to the children's room and found Martha sitting up in bed, shaking. Henry had not disturbed at all and was fast asleep on his back, head to one side and mouth wide open.

"Was it a nasty dream?" she asked.

She knew all about those and their ability to bring terror in the night. She switched on the dim night light that sat on the bedside table and sat on the bed. The light was enough to dispel the darkness and remove the fears that lurked there for the little girl.

The little girl nodded. Beth instinctively put her arm round her. Martha nestled in, still shaking.

"It's all alright now," Beth said softly. "We'll just sit here for a few minutes, shall we? Hold your teddy tight."

Martha nodded again, "I didn't like it," she said, and gradually the shaking lessened.

"I know," Beth said. "It's all gone now."

It only took ten minutes for Beth to realise that the little head had grown heavy against her arm and the breathing had become soft and regular.

"Let's get you snuggled in," she said, and gently eased the little girl back into her sleep position and pulled the duvet round her. She waited a few minutes before returning to her own room, leaving the night light on and their door ajar so that she could listen for a while before letting herself try to sleep again.

It was still feeling right, despite that dramatic interruption, and Beth was able to drift off to sleep again. In fact, it felt just right, but she was too cautious and too scarred to let her optimism run that high.

Chapter Thirteen

Beth's reality check arrived the next morning: Saturday, the day she took over the childcare. Tess came to the kitchen as the children were having their breakfast. She put a set of car keys on the table.

"They're for the Corsa. That's the car we keep for the nanny. It's got child seats fitted and I know the last nanny had just put petrol in it. The garage key is on the same ring."

She then put a bank card on the table. "You can use this for whatever you need. It's contactless. Obviously, that limits what you can spend but you shouldn't need that much."

"Do you know what time you'll be back?" she asked.

"It's always impossible to say. I'll ring you tomorrow afternoon when I know more. You've got my number if you need to get in touch, but you shouldn't have to."

She picked up her handbag and turned to the children. "Come and give Mummy a kiss good-bye……oh, you've got toast and butter on your faces. Never mind, just give me a wave, my darlings."

The children waved and watched her go and Beth's heart ached at the confusion left on their little faces. Mummy had gone and there they were, left with yet another stranger.

With that cursory farewell, Tess was off. Beth imagined she was going to join her husband, although she hadn't actually said that. She sighed; she was in at the deep end. In a way, that was better than being watched over, although she couldn't imagine Tess ever sparing the time to check up too closely on her nannies.

"I wonder if we've got any food for while mummy is away," she said cheerfully.

She checked the fridge and the cupboards and found that there was little to sustain them over the weekend. She checked the freezer and found ample supplies of curly fries, smiley faces and the like, along with turkey twizzlers, fish fingers and chicken nuggets. There was a solitary bag of frozen peas.

"We're going shopping after breakfast," she said. "We need to get some food." There was a Co-op in the village, and she decided that they would walk there.

"After lunch we are going to take Boo to the park."

The children looked at her in surprise.

"Aren't we going to watch the television?" Martha asked.

"Not on a beautiful day like today." She put the dishes in the dishwasher and then, having wiped their hands and faces, lifted them down from their high stools.

"Let's go and put our shoes and coats on," she said, clapping her hands. "I'll chase you upstairs."

The children looked at her in astonishment. "Off you go, I'm coming after you," she said and clapped her hands again and shooed them off. They obeyed and then were amazed as Beth came after them, pretending to chase them. It was fun, but also puzzling because their nannies were never silly, and neither were their mummy and daddy.

As they got ready, she started menu planning and compiling her list in her head. There was no point buying too much food because it was only for the two days, but it was going to be fresh and tasty.

She mastered the alarm system for leaving the house and set off, holding Henry's hand on one side and Martha's on the other. She felt so sorry for them being left with someone they didn't know: someone who was just going to look after them whilst their mother was away for two days and then pass them on to someone else, but they didn't seem bothered.

She chattered away as they walked, pointing out the birds and cats and dogs that they passed. She wasn't used to the continual sound of her own voice, but she could hardly walk along in silence and she wanted them to feel at ease.

She thought they started to enjoy their day and to relax a little as they trundled their little shopping trolleys around the Co-op and dropped the shopping in them. Their highlight was being allowed to unload their shopping on to the conveyor belt. It felt as if Beth was treating them like grown-ups and they relished their responsibility, even though they could hardly reach to put their things on the conveyor. They had been given so much, Beth thought, but they had been deprived of so much more.

They were totally relaxed with her by the time they took Boo to the park that afternoon. They threw the ball for her to fetch and just as she didn't tire, neither did they. It was a joy to hear their peals of laughter as the dog ran back to them each time, wagging her tail.

They were a little concerned that Beth had to clear up after Boo, but were reassured when she explained why as she popped the bag into what she called the special dog bin. They had never had the opportunity of getting to know how to care for the dog that had been bought for them.

They were astonished that Beth let the dog into the kitchen with them when they got home and gave her a bowl of water. She needed it after all that running about and lapped so enthusiastically she splashed droplets on the floor.

"Nanny Brown didn't let Boo in the house," Martha said in amazement at the puddles. "She said she was dirty."

"Well I think she's lovely, and she's not dirty," Beth said. "That's only a drop of water. Your daddy bought her just for you two so, if you think it's a good idea, we can let her live in the house with us whilst I'm here."

"Please," Martha said, and Henry nodded. "But

we must keep her out of Mummy's way when Mummy comes back. Mummy doesn't really like her, though she says she does." She paused for a moment, "Did you know we call her Boo because Harry can't say Boudica?"

Beth noted that Martha called Henry Harry, and he seemed happy with that. It certainly sounded less formal and it suited him.

"I can't say Boudica," he repeated gravely, "so I say Boo," and Beth and Martha both laughed.

"I like Boo," he said. "And I like Beff."

"I like you too, poppet," Beth said, feeling strangely moved at the way the little boy had given her his affection so readily.

Those days with the children gave her a reason to be busy: she was no longer dreaming up things to fill her time and to keep out of Laura's way. Her mind was occupied, and she was no longer fixated on keeping that man and his actions locked from her brain.

She was still insecure and not willing to trust her own judgment. She had never Googled so many things before, as she checked that what they were doing and what they were eating were appropriate for children of their age.

The children never questioned the food she put

in front of them, though she suspected they had rarely eaten fresh vegetables before. They fully approved of the salmon she cooked for them and enjoyed the Greek yoghurt and blueberries.

She had never bathed children before, and she had vague recollections of having to put an elbow in the water to test its temperature, but little else. She wasn't sure if they shared a bath or bathed separately.

She had no need to worry because Martha was full of confidence in the procedure and proceeded to tell her every detail of what had to be done and where everything was. The little girl was, however, rather taken aback afterwards when she was asked to choose a book for their bedtime story. They didn't have bedtime stories, she said, although they did have a lot of books.

"You will tonight, so choose one quickly," Beth said. "The question is, whose bed shall we all sit on tonight for bedtime milk and story?"

"Mine," said Martha. "I'm the oldest. Are we really going to drink our milk in bed?"

Beth nodded.

"Mine," said Harry, a little late but still keen to be involved.

"I wish we could do this ev-er-y night," Martha said as they went downstairs to get their milk.

Beth smiled,"Ev-er-y night would be nice. Do you think Boo will want to listen to our story?"

"In our bedroom?" Harry asked.

"Yes, but not on your beds."

They looked at her as if she had magical powers. They could hardly contain their excitement and they both said it was the best, the very best, bedtime they had ever had.

It was certainly the best bedtime Beth had had for a long time. She was tired because it had been a full-on day, but that was good. It was better than the weariness that often came with inactivity. After she had let the dog out for five minutes, she tried to put the exceptionally complicated alarm on its overnight setting. She pressed the wrong button and spoke, quite by accident, to the person connected to the police link, but that was strangely reassuring. When she had finally set the alarm she went upstairs with the dog at her heels.

She decided it was a good night for a quick bath followed by a long, relaxing read. Boo seemed to be in total agreement and obligingly curled up on the end of her bed to wait for her. It crossed Beth's mind that this could be a lovely way to live.

Chapter Fourteen

Tess telephoned late on Sunday afternoon to say she would be detained and would not be back until Tuesday. She did not ask if Beth would stay on, she just made her statement and rung off. She did not ask after the children and she did not ask how Beth was coping.

Beth was absolutely amazed. She immediately tried to call her back, but the phone went straight to voice mail. After five attempts Beth got the message that Tess had absolutely no intention of speaking to her.

She rang Marie and told her what had happened, and Marie was as shocked as she was. She was sure that if anyone else but Beth had been left in charge they would have called in Social

Services and reported them as abandoned children.

She offered her help, but Beth declined, feeling surprised that she was confident she had things under control.

The children were not the slightest bit worried by their mother's absence, did not question why she'd not wanted to speak to them, weren't worried that she was staying away longer, and they embraced their new regime with joy.

Next morning she thought that they'd enjoy making some cakes for their mother's return and they declared it was the very best thing they had ever done. They were having such fun that she extended their baking session to include some biscuits as well.

They were getting very enthusiastic about scattering flour on the pastry board and rolling the biscuit dough when the doorbell rang. Her stomach lurched as she went to the door, registering that her confidence still had a long way to go. She braced herself to face the visitor, checking through the spy hole first. The old desire for flight was still there but there was nowhere to run.

There was a tall man at the door. She guessed he was in his late thirties, he was immaculately dressed, extremely good looking and carrying an overnight bag.

"You must be a new nanny," he said, as if new nannies were a regular occurrence. "Is Tess here? I'm her brother, Tom. Tom Grace."

"No, she's away," she said. "But I'm just helping out…"

The children had heard his voice and had run into the hall.

"Uncle Tom," they both shrieked, launching themselves at him.

He looked at the two of them with astonishment: they were very floury, and they were very happy. He did not seem at all bothered by the white handprints that appeared on his dark blue trousers and jacket as he hoisted them into the air in turn, nor by the slobbery kisses they planted on his face.

"What are you two up to?"

"We're baking," they chorused.

"Then I'm going to help," he said. "Just give me a minute to get changed and I'll be with you." He turned to Beth, "I didn't know Tess was going away, she never said. Didn't she mention I might come over today?"

Beth was flustered. Her good deed had been trampled all over and now there was a complete stranger, a man she'd never met, expecting to stay the night. It was all a bit too much to absorb.

"No," she replied, unable at that moment to say anything else. Tess had put her in the worst situation imaginable and the old panic was surfacing quickly.

"I'll just get changed," he said, "and then I'm coming to help you bake." He grabbed his bag and bounded upstairs.

He soon joined them in the kitchen and, within minutes, the orderly baking session had become chaotic. Their uncle deliberately got everything wrong. He dropped things, flicked flour at them and generally made a mess. The children were soon even more floury and even more happy.

Tom Grace did not appear threatening in any way so Beth was able to stand back and enjoy the scene. They rolled the dough and tried to use the cutters. Eventually they had a tray of curiously shaped pieces called biscuit bugs to put in the oven.

He watched her as she wiped the excesses off their hands and faces and removed their aprons. A smile spread over his face.

"It's lovely to see them this happy," he said, and there was a sincerity in his voice that touched her heart. It was good to be acknowledged.

"Now, I'd better clear this mess up that I've helped to make."

Beth was astonished. Could this really be Tess Hargreaves' brother? She shook her head to let him know she didn't expect help and started gathering the baking things together. He took no notice of the shake of her head.

"When did you start here?" he asked, running water into the bowl and squirting an extraordinary amount of washing up liquid in so a mountain of bubbles was forming over the bowl.

"Saturday morning," she replied. "But I'm only here so your sister could go to London."

"Oh, I thought you were a new nanny. Are you one of Tess's friends?"

It was embarrassing to explain how she came to be there, so she kept her explanation brief. She could see at once he had read between the lines, and didn't seem impressed.

"She stayed on in London without even asking you?" he asked, and Beth could only nod. There was nothing she could say to make it sound better.

"Did she say what was so urgent in London?"

"I think it was something to do with her husband's promotion," Beth said, realising she actually had no idea.

Tom Grace said nothing, he knew his sister better than Beth did. He had taken a call from Oliver Hargreaves that morning and he had said he was at a finance leaders' conference in Berlin.

"So, let me get this straight. My sister asked you to look after the children for the weekend without actually knowing anything about you? I don't mean to offend you, but that's just unbelievable."

"I think she was desperate," was all Beth could offer.

She felt they had reached a tacit understanding without actually needing to discuss the shortcomings of his sister any further, and he chose not to tell her that Oliver Hargreaves was in Berlin.

"Then this is really embarrassing," Tom Grace said. "I'll stay in the village overnight. I'm sorry about the way I barged in. I had no idea you weren't the new nanny."

Long ago, Beth's naturally polite instincts would have kicked in and she would have said that wasn't necessary. That would have been before that night, so now she was grateful and offered no resistance.

"In fact," he said, "why don't you take a couple

of hours off and I'll put the children to bed this evening?'

"Please, Uncle Tom," Martha said at once. 'But we have a story and a drink of milk in bed now Beth's here."

He looked at Beth and smiled, making it clear the matter was settled and that the story would be read.

Chapter Fifteen

Matthew Thomas was free that evening and was spending it at home. It had only been a few days since she had seen him, but he looked different. His skin was greyer, and his eyes more troubled than she had ever seen.

It came as a shock to Beth, and she asked at once how he was and what was the matter.

"I'm tired, that's all," he replied.

"Are you sure that's all?" She was anxious.

He sighed, "I've been wondering if I'm doing any good here. I might be more use somewhere else."

Alarm swept over her. "You're needed here," she said, "really needed."

He understood her response was about her and smiled to reassure her.

"As I said, I'm probably just tired. I've had a few call-outs in the night this week. My older parishioners have been leaving this world in the early hours." The smile didn't quite give warmth to his eyes, but Beth was reassured, mainly because she wanted to be.

They ordered pizza and opened a bottle of wine. It was good for them both to spend some time together, and he was pleased to see how positive she seemed.

She told him about what had happened at the Hargreaves' and he shared her amazement and indignation at Tess's callousness. He offered no comment or opinion on what she might be doing, even though he thought she it was possible she wasn't with her husband.

He sat back and listened as she talked about the children, noting her animation and also noticing that she was eating far more than usual as she talked. It struck him that, even though she was annoyed, she was actually enjoying being with the children and faint alarm bells rang in his head. He didn't want Tess Hargreaves ensnaring her further, but he said nothing at that point.

They settled to watch a film on Netflix and finish the bottle they had opened. Matthew had matters niggling away and didn't seem to be able to sit still, paying little attention to the film.

"Are you really feeling unsettled?" she asked.

"It's just that I don't feel challenged," he said. "I didn't become a priest to feel comfortable, and that's exactly how I feel here."

"The people in the village love you," she said. "They say you're the best thing that's happened in the parish for years."

"Again, I didn't become a priest to become popular," he said. "Anyway, as I said, I'm very tired and I may not be thinking straight."

"You've still got the centre," she added.

She had inadvertently touched a nerve. "I am needed there," he admitted. "There's so much to do. There is a new volunteer though, which helps. His name is Stefan and he's starting to make a difference. He tackles all the heavy jobs."

"Then I hope he stays because you look as if you need the help," she said.

He turned to look at her more carefully, "You, on the other hand, look much better."

"It's the children. They had the most pathetic little lives and they seem so much happier already."

"Be careful, Beth. They're not your responsibility and I understand Tess Hargreaves is quite ruthless. I know she's fired a few nannies on a whim, and she could easily see you as a convenient replacement. I wouldn't like to see you get sucked in."

His words surprised her. She had just started to feel positive and he was sounding wary. It wasn't like him to be remotely critical of anyone, though, if she was honest, he had hardly been harsh about Tess. He had always tried to get her to be more upbeat and positive, and now he was counselling caution. She realised that he would have his own reasons.

She had a lot to think about as she walked back to The Willows. It bothered her that Matthew had seemed so down, and it bothered her even more that he wasn't feeling settled in the village. She knew he enjoyed the challenge of the work at the centre, and she suspected that, in comparison, his parish duties seemed mundane. He'd seemed pleased with the new volunteer so maybe Stefan would make a real difference there once he'd settled in properly and Matthew might start to feel better.

She was stunned by his warning about Tess Hargreaves. She hadn't thought beyond Tess's return. She had to take it seriously because she was sure he had only been trying to forewarn her.

She'd originally imagined that she would keep the children happy in Tess's absence, then go back to her old routine. It wasn't too much of a stretch to imagine Tess asking her to stay on, and she had to admit that it had crossed her mind as well.

Marie had teased her and called her Mary Poppins. That night she didn't feel too much like Mary Poppins, she had become aware that she needed to be totally sure about what she wanted to do next, regardless of what might suit Tess Hargreaves.

It was temporarily elating to exchange a few words with Tom, Tess's brother, when she got in. He was ready to head off on her return but paused long enough to update her. He told her the children hadn't stopped talking about her and what they'd been up to with her, and he took great pains to tell her how much happier they seemed.

"I'll tell Tess how lucky she is that you helped her out," he concluded. "Those poor children have had some real harridans looking after them recently."

When he left, she felt a new feeling settle inside her, as if somehow, despite Matthew's warning, she had become the route to the two little ones' happiness. It felt good to have a purpose.

She collected Boo, set the alarm and went to bed. There was a lot going on in her mind that night.

Chapter Sixteen

Tom Grace reappeared as the children were eating their breakfast and again, he absorbed the change in them with pleasure. They were only making suggestions about what they could do that morning, but it was clear they were now open to possibilities other than television and were bursting with ideas.

"Have you heard from Tess?" he asked.

Beth shook her head.

"She hasn't been picking up my calls either," he said.

He proposed taking the children out for the morning and said he would be staying on until Tess returned. Beth sensed he had things to say to his sister but made no comment.

"I'm going to take you to soft play," he said. He was clearly used to visiting and taking the children out. "If you want to pack your things and get away, it's fine. I'll be here until tonight."

She was in the strangest position because she felt responsible for Martha and Harry, and it felt wrong to just hand them over to their uncle. Her common sense told her they would be fine with him, and that Tess could hardly object because she'd literally abandoned her two little ones to a stranger, whereas she was only letting them go out with their uncle.

"Don't feel you have to stay on here," he said. "I need be here when Tess gets back. There are a few things I want to say to her, and I'd rather we were alone for that conversation when she finally puts in an appearance."

It made sense, and so she said her goodbyes to Martha and Harry as they left for soft play and then packed up her few bits and pieces into her bag. She could carry it so easily that she felt slightly guilty that she'd let Matthew give her a lift on the Friday evening. She would be glad of the exercise. She walked back to Laura's, realising that she did not want to go back there.

Tom was furious with his sister, though he would never let his niece and nephew see the mood he was in and he mulled everything over as he sat with a cup of coffee whilst the children ran around the soft play centre.

He tried Tess's number, but the call went straight to voicemail each time, so then he called Oliver Hargreaves, who did pick up. They had a long chat, and Tom made it clear what he'd found at The Willows and that things had got to change for the children's sake.

Oliver had always been a long-distance father. Tom suspected he rarely stayed over at The Willows now, but that was none of his concern at that moment. His only interest was the welfare of those children and he had to make Oliver see that things were not right and get him to do something to change them. He knew that Oliver controlled the purse strings and that that alone was enough leverage to make Tess listen.

He finished the call with a sigh. This was the last thing he wanted to be doing, going behind his sister's back and giving her husband instructions, but he had no choice. Neither parent was prioritising their children.

He was not looking forward to confronting his sister.

Chapter Seventeen

Beth, the girl who once tried to ensure there was nothing left to tell the world she'd ever been there, and had tried to end her life, suddenly had decisions to face. She had gone from not caring where she was to knowing that she had to make changes. She couldn't stay on at Laura's. She had to find some-where else to live, and she had her budding accoun-tancy business to build, but somehow, she couldn't get the children out of her head.

She stashed her things away and then put Samson's lead on and took him for an extremely long walk. She had hoped to clear her mind but that was impossible. She was coping with a jumble of emotions, but most strident was the knowledge that she had felt more alive and happier with Tess

Hargreaves' children than she ever thought possible.

"Maybe," she thought, "helping them would be a good way of helping myself."

She couldn't explain it beyond that, but it seemed to make sense.

Tess, in the meantime, had arrived home at just after two. The children had had their lunch and had gone for a nap, absolutely worn out by their time at the huge soft play centre they had visited.

She was a little surprised to see her brother's car there, having completely forgotten he was due to make a visit after the weekend. She dropped her Louis Vuitton weekend bag carelessly on to the hall floor and went into the kitchen.

She looked around. "Where's….?" She snapped her fingers expressively as she realised she couldn't remember Beth's name.

It was the final straw for Tom, who had been seething since he had found out she had gone off and left her children with a stranger. She'd not even attempted to make any checks on her.

"You don't even know her name, do you?" he said. His voice was angry but controlled.

She ignored that.

"Where are the children?" Her question was asked so casually it enraged him further.

It would serve her right, he thought, if Beth Anderson had run away with them or had consigned them to Social Services, but he knew he didn't mean that. The children had always been his priority and he had come to realise, finally and sadly, that that was not true of either of their parents.

He had a lot of ground to cover with her whilst her children napped. He knew it was no use ranting at her, even though he thought she deserved it, because she would just switch off and he would end up disturbing Martha and Harry.

"You are damned lucky you chose someone so reliable or you could have ended up with the children being taken into care,"

She laughed in his face, as though she knew she had selected the best person possible to look after them and he was being totally ridiculous. He made her sit down and he tried to make her see that things had to change, that the children needed stability. A stream of unsuitable nannies who either got fired or walked out was doing them harm.

She tried several times to interrupt, but she saw it was pointless. He cut her dead each time. She had never seen him so angry and even she realised she was not going to bluster her way out of this situation. She momentarily thought of asking him what the hell her children had to do with him, but she shrunk from going that far, and then was relieved she'd not asked.

He wanted greater clarity over their father's commitment to them. He wanted to know if he ever came home just to spend time with them. Tess was reluctant to answer, knowing that, in replying, she would have to reveal the chinks in her marriage, but he gave her no choice.

The answers were unsatisfactory to Tom. Oliver only popped in to see them on constituency surgery days or when he had constituency meetings. As for his relationship with Tess, he still made sure that both of them were highly visible at major local events and photo opportunities, but he never actually stayed at the house.

Tom Grace was no fool. He knew his sister needed to be the centre of attention and an empty marriage, despite all the advantages and social connections it brought, was soul-destroying. He realised how miserable she must feel inside, and what a good job she was doing keeping it well-hidden, but that did not excuse her neglect of the children. He could not allow her to paint herself into the role of a tragic heroine, though she did give it a try.

"So, where did you go?" he asked, knowing she would be unaware he had been speaking to Oliver.

"London, I'm sure you know that already."

"Be honest with me, Tess. Oliver was in Berlin, so what was so important that you had to dash away and leave Martha and Harry?"

There was silence. That was the conversation Tess was not prepared to have. Tom was afraid she was having an affair that could lead her to abandon the children altogether. He knew their father would not be taking over if she did. He had to know her plans.

"Are you thinking of leaving Oliver?"

"No, not at the moment," she replied, but that was not enough to ease his anxiety.

It was a long and painful conversation, but Tom Grace had one clear and unwavering intention. She had to make a solemn undertaking that she would find a nanny who was both competent and caring, and then make the arrangement work. Beyond that, he didn't really care if she wanted to spend time with the lover she wouldn't admit to.

"I'll talk to that girl," she said. "You said that Martha and Henry loved her and that she was good with them."

"Her name is Beth, and she's an accountant, not a nanny. And, by the way, unlike you, she soon learnt to call your son Harry to please him. You can't expect her to just move in here and do child minding because it suits you. You couldn't even remember her name."

Tess was insistent she was going to ask Beth, emphasising how she had always known she would be excellent, and Tom was becoming more and more frustrated with her.

"Until you have someone in place who I approve of, I am staying on," he said at last. "No arguments. And Oliver agrees things have to change."

She looked at him in astonishment, realising that there was no way she could work on him to change his mind. She was horrified to hear that he had Oliver on his side. She had always been able to wheedle her way around him in the past but she knew she had pushed him too far this time. She could not risk upsetting her husband either, because, although he was generous, he could easily withdraw her access to the funds her lifestyle required.

She would, she decided, work her charms on that girl.

Chapter Eighteen

Tess phoned the next morning to make sure Beth was working at the cafe and turned up an hour later with a full-on charm offensive and a huge bouquet of flowers.

She was gushing in her thanks and her praise for all that Beth had done and asked her to have a cup of coffee with her. Beth sat down with her and Tess got fully into her flow, explaining that Beth had made such a tremendous impact on her children that she just had to ask if there was any way Beth might consider caring for them full time.

She went into elaborate details about the generous pay, the highest they'd ever offered because she was so special, and how she would be more like a member of the family than an employee because the children were so fond of her.

Beth did not for one minute believe that this woman had developed a sudden devotion to her. She knew only too well that Tom had had to get her out of the way the previous day so he could speak his mind to her. She had also learnt the hard way that Tess was not a good or reliable employer.

She let the wave of flattery wash over her because she already knew that she wanted to work with Martha and Harry. She had talked her thoughts through with both Marie and Matthew and she knew that they both thought she was crazy to even consider working for Tess. However, she had realised how happy she had felt being with the children and she wanted more of that in her life after all she had been through, even if she had to toughen up and learn how to handle Tess.

She knew she wanted to get away from Laura's house, but she also knew that that was not the reason she was considering taking this job. She'd already discovered that she was strong enough to make that move, no matter what. It was a happy coincidence that The Willows was her old home and had seemed, in her mind, to welcome her back like an old friend.

"I know you're an accountant," Tess was saying, "and I know I shouldn't be asking you, because that's a really great profession, but you have special skills and I would love you to be able to put them to good use."

Beth had no time for more of her flattery and persuasion so she thanked her and said, quite emphatically, that she would give it some thought and, if she was interested she would want a contract detailing her hours and her rate of pay, holiday entitlement and conditions of sick pay.

She was proud of that. She had already worked out what she would say if the need arose because she had no intention of appearing or being a push-over. She enjoyed the way it stopped Tess in her onslaught of flattery and her lists of reasons why she simply had to agree. She'd placed it all on a business footing and that was how she wanted it to be.

"So, when will you decide?"

"I'll let you know by the end of the week. I'll have a lot to think over when I receive the contract," she said, "and thank you for the flowers."

Chapter Nineteen

There was never any doubt in Beth's mind that she would take the job, even though she had listened to Marie and Matthew's opinions and fully understood their concerns. She just wanted to spend time with Martha and Harry and let their enthusiasm and innocence wash over her and bring some warmth back into her life. She had felt that much-needed glow when she had provided cover that weekend and she wanted more.

It was good to move her things into a room that really did feel like her own. She invested the money Tess had paid her for her previous stint into a laptop, thinking she could still keep up with a few accounting jobs whilst the children were in bed. She had two evenings free each week which she had arranged to spend with Matthew, but, apart from that, her free time was entirely uncommitted.

To be fair, working for Tess worked out better than she anticipated. Tess did take off regularly for a couple of days but proved reliable about her returns. She also started to take more meals with the children and was engaging with them a little more. Beth knew it was because it was easier for her to eat what she had cooked fresh than have to pick something up from Waitrose or Marks and Spencer to microwave.

Beth rarely saw Oliver Hargreaves. He was a handsome man, always immaculately dressed and he had that confident, entitled air of someone who had had a privileged upbringing and education. He would drop in either before or after his monthly surgeries in the constituency office, or when he had a local engagement, and would spend half an hour with the children.

She noted that Tess always contrived to be out of the house when he visited, unless her attendance at a function was required. On these occasions she assumed the role of devoted wife, as if she lived her life in total adoration of her man and was proud to be hanging on to his arm.

Beth's greatest joys came through the time she

spent alone with the children. They were madly enthusiastic about the activities she sorted out for them and their happiest times were spent around the kitchen table painting, model making, printing or drawing.

The huge fridge was soon adorned with artwork held on by magnets, which they had chosen themselves. It started to look like a place where children lived and played rather than just passed through. Tess eventually got used to admiring their efforts, and faithfully echoed Beth's reactions. She did it so well the children were convinced she appreciated their work as much as Beth did.

They went out every day for a walk with Boo, allowing Tess to dispense with the services of The Dogman very quickly. What with Beth providing her meals and no longer having to pay him, her disposable income had perked up.

The children thrived on the outdoor life and it meant that they were always ready for bed because they had had plenty of exercise and fresh air. Beth noticed that after a few days neither of them asked to watch television. They were always too busy.

When a national newspaper wanted to do a feature on the home life of the Hargreaves for their Sunday supplement Beth got them organised. Tess and Oliver both slid, seamlessly and immaculately dressed, into the tableaux that Beth had set up for them. Tess and the children pretended to make gingerbread men and Oliver and the children pretended to work on the space rockets Beth had started for them.

The Hargreaves slid, equally seamlessly and immaculately dressed, out of these scenes and went to pose with Boo and the children for more photographs in the garden. Beth cleared up their debris and the irony of this made her smile.

The pictures of domestic bliss proved so successful that a society magazine did an in-depth feature on the 'Harmonious Hargreaves' that led to Tess being offered a column, with a ghost writer, as their childcare agony aunt. She declined because of previous commitments but she was sorely tempted. This amused Beth. The only commitments Tess had were her trips to London and her get-togethers with her cronies.

Beth, whilst aware of these ironies, was actually becoming more content and at ease with herself. The day-to-day life the three of them lived, away from the parents, was stress-free and happy. She didn't expect either Hargreaves to acknowledge she had been the basis for their successes in the media and they didn't disappoint.

Beth wasn't doing this job for recognition of her skills with Martha and Harry. She was doing it because she had wanted to set them free from their limited and restrictive lives and give them some joy. She also knew, beyond that, they were proving to be part of her route to recovery. Their affection for her was more uplifting than any drug the psychiatrists had ever prescribed for her. When they ran and gave her a hug, she felt a joy she had thought she had lost for ever.

She loved bedtime the most. They absolutely adored her stories and made it absolutely clear to their mother that, on Beth's nights off, story time was non-negotiable. They loved the silly voices she adopted when reading in character. Their laughter was the boost her damaged self badly needed. It made her smile when they told her their mummy was no good at voices but she did her best.

Their lives settled into a comfortable and cosy pattern and Beth felt as though her existence was starting to have a direction. She was able to plan ahead for the first time since the attack. It was only the on-line shopping order for the next week or booking tickets for the children's farm they loved so much, but she could look forward and no longer be engulfed with terror.

It did her good to be back in her old home and to see it come alive with laughter again. It had looked immaculate and stylish on her first visit, but sterile too. Now it felt like a home again, somewhere she actually belonged. The Willows was helping her recovery too.

Tom Grace made regular visits and she loved to see the children hurl themselves at him when he arrived and shower him with hugs. When she heard them telling him what they had been doing she knew her efforts were working. They too were enjoying their days.

Life was always a little easier for her when he was around. He arrived wanting to take the children out, play with them and read them stories. He expected to be left alone with them so she didn't have to be in his company. This helped her. Her recovery was coming along but it not so advanced that she was at ease with him.

Beth started to think how sad it was that Oliver and Tess did not get the same pleasure from spending time with Martha and Harry that she and Tom did.

Chapter Twenty

It was not a totally Utopian existence for Beth: it was real life so there were ups and downs. The children squabbled and made friends again, they fell down and scraped their knees and elbows, they got upset tummies and, towards the end of summer, they got coughs and colds.

Beth took them to the surgery but was reassured that their chests were clear and there was nothing to worry about so, when she caught their germs she didn't give it a second thought. She took paracetamol and dosed herself with cough linctus and carried on as usual.

It was only when her cough was getting worse and she could hear herself wheezing that she got herself a phone appointment. It had to be with the nurse practitioner as the doctors were fully booked.

The nurse listened to her story and assured her she was doing exactly the right things. She pointed out that the village was rife with this particular virus and that the classes in the primary school were half empty. She said it usually took at least a week to clear.

Beth hated fuss of any kind, so she left it at that and soldiered on. It was difficult because she wasn't sleeping: as soon as she lay down her symptoms worsened and she ended up having to sit up in bed most of the night to ease her coughing and wheezing.

She had been up in the night with the children several times over the previous couple of weeks and that compounded her tiredness. She hardly knew how she dragged herself to the Saturday when Tom Grace was due to visit and take over so she could have a day off.

That day she was practically gasping for breath between coughing bouts as she made the children's breakfast and, in despair, she asked if Tess would mind taking over. Tess, irritated by the constant coughing, agreed, having checked her watch to confirm that her brother was less than an hour away, so help was close at hand.

Beth took a glass of water upstairs with her and got back into bed with relief. When she felt her forehead it was burning, but she had had her dose of paracetamol so there was nothing more she could do for at least another four hours. She just wanted unbroken sleep but knew that was unlikely.

She texted Matthew to let him know she wouldn't be meeting him at lunchtime and, after putting her phone on silent, lay back on her pile of pillows: it was still impossible to lie flat. She was vaguely aware of the household noises in the distance as she drifted in and out of sleep. She registered the arrival of Tom Grace and his departure with Harry and Martha, but otherwise she only disturbed when her cough took hold.

The day became a hazy, blank fog and she had to fight to leave the mists behind when she became vaguely aware of someone tugging at her arm. Eventually she managed to focus her eyes and, through the clearing fog, she could make out Harry's little face.

"Beff won't wake up," Harry said to his uncle, who had taken them upstairs for their bedtime routine.

Tom Grace went to her door and tapped gently. When there was no reply he peeped round the door. He could hear Beth's rattly breathing then and when he saw her, beige faced, lying against her pillow mountain he felt alarmed.

"Beth," he said, going in. "Beth!" he repeated, this time more loudly.

She struggled once again to fight her way through her fog to open her eyes. She tried to say hello, but her coughing started and the rattling, bubbling noise got worse.

"Martha, go and fetch Mummy," he called to the other room, "quickly please."

He took his phone from his pocket and dialled 999 and Tess appeared as he started describing Beth's condition to the emergency services. She reacted straight away, taking the children into their room to get them into their pyjamas, not wanting them to be frightened.

"You stay with Beth," she called to Tom, leaving him free to continue his conversation. "We're fine."

It took about twenty minutes for a paramedic to arrive, with the ambulance only five minutes behind.

Tom hovered by the door as they assessed her condition. He overheard their remarks as they worked, and he felt his anxiety rising. He could see she was vaguely aware of them but was largely unresponsive.

When they fitted the heart monitor they were as shocked to see the ugly scarring across her chest, but, having registered it, they carried on. Old scars had nothing to do with her present condition.

Tom was stunned at the sight of them. He turned his head away, knowing it was something he was never meant to see, but its image seared into his brain.

"We're going to have to take her into hospital," they said, and even more activity broke out. One fetched a carry chair whilst the other stashed their gear away and unhooked her from the heart monitor ready for transfer. The paramedic completed the paperwork whilst all this was going on.

Tess appeared in the doorway to see how things were going and Tom asked if she wanted to go with Beth. She shook her head, so he resolved to go.

"See if you can get in touch with that priest she sees," Tom said. "Let him know what's happened."

He watched them negotiate Beth down the stairs and then followed them.

As he closed the door behind him he could hear both children crying upstairs. He realised they would be scared, but their mother was with them and Beth, though unaware of it, needed someone from The Willows to be with her right then. After all she had done for the children, it was no time to appear uncaring.

The ambulance men delivered Beth straight into one of the emergency rooms and completed the handover.

"Hope she goes on alright mate," one of them said to Tom.

"So do I," he replied, with total sincerity.

He was shown to a waiting area whilst the medics got to work to stabilise, diagnose and start treating Beth. He was left to his own thoughts. As always, they centred on the children's welfare, which was so much improved, but he was also genuinely anxious for Beth.

He had been waiting for about an hour when Matthew Thomas arrived, a picture of flustered anxiety. All Tom could do was relay what had happened. It felt woefully inadequate to admit that Harry had found her poorly at bedtime and that no one had checked up on her since breakfast.

He had no medical update for Matthew other than what he had overheard from the ambulance staff, and that was worrying enough for both of them.

Updates over, they lapsed into silence because there was nothing more to say. They both jumped to their feet when a doctor came and led them to a small room to bring them up to date.

He explained that Beth had developed pneumonia and that her condition must have deteriorated dramatically for her to become so ill so fast. He explained that she would need to to be admitted and remain on oxygen. He told them he had already started her on intravenous antibiotics and a course of steroids.

Beth was to be moved within minutes to a ward and they would then be able to see her very briefly. The doctor said that he hoped that Beth would respond quickly to the treatment regime, but he expected her to be in hospital for the next few days.

He paused for questions but neither had

anything to ask so he took his leave and left them to absorb the news.

"Sounds positive," Tom observed.

Matthew did not reply. To him it sounded awful and he was annoyed beyond words that Beth had got into such a state before anyone found her and sought assistance. He couldn't confront that right then, but he knew it would have to be faced later.

They were glad to be collected by a nurse and taken to the ward where Beth was. She was in a single room, right next to the nursing station and was attached to a variety of drips and machines. The nurse assured them that it looked more frightening than it really was, and the machines were there to monitor her so that they could respond to any changes.

Both were shocked at how tiny and ill Beth looked as she lay there in her hospital gown resting against the raised pillows.

Matthew spoke first and she fought to open her eyes and focus on him. She managed a smile and he squeezed her hand very gently. "What a pickle you've got yourself in," he said affectionately. She managed a very weak squeeze back and he felt a wave of relief sweep over him that she knew him and had registered what he said.

Tom Grace stayed at some distance from her bed and simply told her to get well. He had no other message. He was so reliant on her for Martha and Harry's wellbeing that her health was of primary importance to him. He left so that Matthew could have a moment with Beth alone.

Matthew was glad that Tom Grace had slipped away. He took her free hand again, raised it to his lips and kissed it so very gently and tenderly she did not notice. The nurse returned too soo as far as he was concerned, and he had to leave.

The men met again in the corridor and left the ward armed with information on visiting times and ward phone numbers. Matthew left his number for emergency contact.

"Can I give you a lift home?" Matthew asked. He was uneasy that this man had come with Beth in the ambulance and was uncomfortable about his motivation. He knew that was because, each day, he had to face just how strong his feelings for Beth were and he had no wish for a rival.

Tom Grace had one desire: he wanted Beth to continue caring for Martha and Harry and he had no wish for her to run away with this priest, who was so clearly besotted with her. He wondered if Beth was aware of the intensity of his feelings and he wondered if Matthew knew of the deep scarring she carried on her chest.

He accepted the lift. It would have been foolish not to at that time of night and he hoped to open up the subject of what he had seen, yet what his brain could not compute.

He wasn't sure if Matthew was bound to keep the secrets of the confessional because he had never had any interest whatsoever in religion. He hadn't a clue which priest did what. All he discovered on that journey back to the village was that Matthew did know about the scars. He was giving nothing further away, whatever he knew.

Tom accepted that what he had seen would niggle away like a worm in his brain and that there was little chance of getting rid of it. He had never seen such vicious scarring and his imagination was tortured as he tried to account for it.

Chapter Twenty-One

Three people spent time that night wondering how quickly Beth would recover and how her convalescence and the care of the children could be managed.

Tess Hargreaves regarded it as a matter of great inconvenience. Things had been going so well, better than she could remember. One thing was absolutely clear to her. She was no nurse and she would not be running up and downstairs looking after Beth. If she couldn't look after herself there was no question of her returning there.

The children were a different matter. She wasn't clear how long Beth would take to recover but she knew it was going to be too long for her to manage without help. She was aware she could ask her cleaner to help out where she could, but she would never be persuaded to let her regular customers down.

There was no chance of her husband coming home for a full weekend, let alone longer, so he wasn't the answer. She knew she could wheedle Tom into working from The Willows for a few days, but he couldn't do that and look after the children at the same time.

She realised she would just have to ring the agency, no matter what Tom said, and she also realised he would expect her to keep Beth on and not replace her.

She wondered briefly if Beth would have somewhere to go to convalesce but she had no way of knowing the answer, so she pushed those thoughts away. She needed to sleep, not worry about someone else.

Tom Grace knew his sister would want the children looked after, and he knew there was no way she would look after Beth on her release from hospital. He was, as always, totally honest in his analysis. It wasn't too much to expect his sister to care for her own children for a short time, given the circumstances, but he knew that was not going to happen. He also knew she would definitely not be taking Beth's care under her control.

He hated the thought of Beth alone on the top floor, dragging herself about to get something to eat and drink. There was no way he could let that happen: she might decide that this was such an uncaring household she had to leave. He couldn't see a realistic solution unless he gave himself some clear time off work. He knew at once that this would mean he'd be looking in on Beth as well as caring for the children, and he couldn't imagine her wanting him popping in and out. She gave off clear signals of her boundaries and he knew he was tolerated but not welcomed.

It shamed him that all he wanted was to make sure Beth didn't give up on caring for Martha and Harry. He knew the only way of making that happen was to take some of the weight off his sister: someone in that house had to take on responsibility and it wouldn't be Tess. The timing, in terms of work, could not have been worse but, after all she'd done for the children, Beth had nearly died alone upstairs. She was an excellent nanny, good for the children but she could easily decide she had had enough and go back to accountancy. He could not risk that.

He also spent a long time thinking about her scars. He could still see them when he closed his eyes. He knew from his sister that there was a history of a psychiatric illness in her background somewhere, but he couldn't believe she'd self-mutilated. He'd heard a bit about self harm, but, on reflection, he couldn't believe she would ever have chosen that word. He also doubted it was possible for her to inflict that carving on herself. She'd have had to do it in mirror writing. So what had she been through in the past?

Of course, he suspected the priest knew exactly what had happened to her, but he couldn't ask again. It would be too insensitive. Anyway, the secrets of the confessional, if that were his thing, would keep him sworn to silence. He still didn't know if Matthew Thomas heard confessions, but he was certain he knew Beth's secrets and would never betray them.

Tom Grace did not sleep that night.

Matthew knew what he wanted to do but it was totally impossible. He wanted to take her back to the vicarage and take care of her himself, but he could never do that. He had to find a way to get her the care and space she needed to recover properly, but he simply did not know how.

He knew one thing, however willing Laura might be to undertake her care, and he was sure she would be, Beth would never return to the little house she had been so anxious to leave.

Another thing was absolutely clear: the decision to leave the parish and take up the bishop's offer of full-time urban ministry, working at the day centre, would have to wait until Beth was better. He had known for some time how he felt about her, though he had not allowed himself to dwell on it, but that night he knew that she was all that mattered to him.

Beth was unaware of all this thinking that was going on. She was sleeping the deep sleep of rampant infection, with regular unwelcome interruptions into her feverish dreams when staff did her hourly observations. She was oblivious to everything else.

Chapter Twenty-Two

Beth was disturbed early the next morning, as patients in hospital always are. It was confusing. She could remember feeling ill, she could remember struggling for breath but, after that, she had no clear recollection of the actual events that led to her hospitalisation. She thought she could remember Harry's anxious little face and she had vague memories of people wearing face masks looming over her and asking her questions, but their voices had been distorted and she had not made sense of any of it.

She assessed her situation. Her chest was tight and sore, but the excruciating pain and the fighting for breath had stopped. She had a cannula in her hand that was attached to a bag of clear fluid, hanging from a drip stand. She was wired up to a machine by the side of her bed displaying her vital signs. She had an oxygen mask on, she was in a hospital gown and was lying in a bed in a soulless little room.

"Toast or cereal?" the woman in the grey uniform asked, as she popped her head round the door. There was no ceremony in her approach.

"Toast," Beth replied automatically, unsure if she would ever eat again.

She was amazed that before the toast that she positively did not want had arrived, Matthew came in smiling and carrying a small bag.

"A dog collar opens many doors," he said as if in explanation. "I wore it specially to gain access to you." He took hold of her free hand as he sat in the high-backed plastic chair that was beside her bed.

He looked the epitome of a kindly vicar and so full of concern for her that her eyes filled with grateful tears.

He was able to explain what had happened and how she came to be there. She was astonished that she had become so ill so quickly, and thankful that Tom Grace had found her and acted so fast.

He had sorted out getting a few things for her when he dropped Tom Grace off in the early hours of that morning. He was no expert on women's requirements, and he hadn't wanted to pry through her things, so he had asked for Tess's help and had picked up the bag that morning. She had remembered toothpaste and toothbrush, comb, slippers, a couple of nightdresses and underwear. He had reminded her to pack Beth's mobile phone and charger.

She looked in the bag with a rising sense of embarrassment that Tess, the woman who even had designer rubber gloves, had looked through her drawers, but at least it meant she could wear her own things. The thought of Tess picking through her multi-pack supermarket underwear was excruciatingly embarrassing, but she was grateful to have it.

He wanted to bombard her questions about how she felt, how she had slept and how much discomfort she was in, but he held back. She had not seen a doctor that morning and had nothing to tell him. He actually knew more than she did, and he had to tell her about her pneumonia and treatment. No matter what they spoke of during that visit, his overwhelming feeling was one of relief to see her awake and safe.

He assured her he had the visiting times and would return that evening. He didn't want to outstay the ten minutes the ward sister had allowed him, so he squeezed her hand again and left.

Modern practices do not indulge patients. After she had removed the uneaten toast, the grey garbed woman reappeared and went through the door that led to the bathroom and came back with a bowl of water. She helped herself to the bag of toiletries and towel that Matthew had delivered and proceeded to assist Beth to wash and dry her face and handed her her toothbrush, charged with toothpaste. She negotiated Beth through the procedure of transferring from hospital gown to her own nightdress, sorting out cables and tubes as they went along

Beth was glad to be a little fresher and to have her own nightdress on, but most of all, she was glad to lie back on to her pillows and refit the oxygen mask. She was exhausted.

The doctors did their rounds later that morning. Her doctor had the same brisk and efficient manner he had had with Matthew the previous night, but his explanations were clear and his instructions were simple.

He said that she had been very ill because her oxygen levels had dropped so low. He reported that the readings were improving now, and the antibiotics appeared to have taken hold of the infection overnight, so her recovery promised to be straightforward. He told her she would be in hospital for at least three or four days so they could ensure her recovery was on track.

And then he was off to the next patient, leaving Beth to absorb the information he had given her. She could hear every word he said in the next room and she tried not to listen, aware that their conversation had also been widely overheard. She was too tired to care.

His information had complemented what Matthew had told her and she understood her situation perfectly. Her main worry was that she would not be able to care for the children for a couple of weeks and she was slightly anxious if that meant she'd not be able to have the use of her room.

Her fears were allayed by a visit from Tom Grace that afternoon. He came into the room carrying a selection of magazines. She was surprised to see him but was grateful for his concern and the reassurances he brought.

"Don't be silly," he said when she asked if she could go back to her room when she was discharged. "We can't let you go off somewhere on your own. We need to make sure you're O.K.

You're the best thing that has happened to those two: they've gone from being little robots to happy young rascals."

She was pleased by his reassurance and glad that he had seen and approved of their transformation.

"Who will look after them whilst I am out of action?" she asked.

"We're working on that," he said. "I'm staying on for a while," a smile spread over his face, "and it's not that unreasonable to expect my sister to cope occasionally on her own. But what about you and your care?"

"I'll only be here for a couple more days," she said, "but I'll be able to manage when I leave. It's only day one and I'm already so much better. If I take my time I will be able to potter about and take care of myself. I think I'll need rest more than anything."

He looked at her closely. She looked totally washed out, but she was alert and following their conversation. "I'll be fine," she said. "I've been through worse."

He thought immediately of the scars he'd seen and wondered, as he had done at least a hundred times since, if he ought to tell her that he had seen them. He felt she had a right to know but it was not going to crop up in conversation.

"It's good of you to visit," she said. "I really didn't expect to see you."

"It's good of you to be so calm. You have every right to be angry at the way you were ignored yesterday."

"I wasn't ignored," she said. "I told your sister I needed to go to bed. I didn't give her any reason to be concerned."

"She could have looked in on you at the very least," he said. "Don't misunderstand me, I love my sister, but you and I both know what she's like." He smiled, "And, as always, you are the soul of tact."

He looked thoughtful, and then he spoke from the heart. "You already know that those two children are the most important things in my life. I feel I have to keep my eye on them, to watch out for them." He didn't elaborate on his reasons although they both knew he had plenty of them.

He didn't stay longer as he could see she was getting tired. He wrote his number down on her menu sheet and told her to call if she needed anything.

Matthew Thomas visited her early that evening. He seemed slightly irritated that Tom Grace had already been to see her that afternoon, but he was glad that Beth had been reassured by his visit.

When he had heard her health update he was sure, despite what she said, she'd struggle on her discharge from hospital. She certainly deserved some care. He had no proposals to put forward because he dared not suggest that she should stay with Laura.

"I've checked with Tom Grace and I can go back there when I'm discharged."

She saw the look of concern cross his face.

"Don't worry. I'm breathless and very tired now, but I'll be able to look after myself by then. You don't get spoiled in hospital."

"I wish you could come and stay with me at the vicarage," he said. "I'd love you to come, but you understand why I can't ask?"

"Of course," she said.

She looked at his kind face and she felt so grateful to him for the loving care that he showed that her heart lurched a little. She would have loved to have been able to stay with him, and she could not imagine her life without his support.

Chapter Twenty-Three

Beth had a visit from Laura very soon after her discharge from hospital and it became obvious very quickly that the woman had an agenda far beyond checking on her wellbeing.

Laura observed the pleasantries of enquiring after her health in her brisk manner before she embarked on her real purpose.

"You really are such a selfish bitch," she said. "I know you've been very ill, but you even try to turn pneumonia to your advantage."

Beth had never warmed to Laura but the venom behind her words stung and what she said made no sense at all. She didn't reply. Laura, having started her rehearsed speech, continued with renewed enthusiasm.

"No wonder you couldn't wait to leave my house so that you could come to this swanky place but let me tell you that mine is paid for. I own every brick. The Hargreaves only rent this place, you know. Two-penny-halfpenny millionaires!"

She looked to see the effect her words were having on Beth, but this onslaught got no reaction. Beth had grown up in The Willows and her parents still owned it, but that was her business, not Laura's. She also knew Laura had actually inherited her house and had not paid for it.

"Matthew is a man of God," she stormed on. "He has a vocation and you are making him compromise his work for the Lord."

These words did strike home. As far as Beth was aware Matthew had been considering his future and had to make a decision, but she was not remotely aware that she played a part in his deliberations.

"You've got him wrapped round your finger. He puts serving you before everything, even his vocation," she said, "and he doesn't realise what a manipulative little bitch you really are. You flutter your eyelashes and play at being so very needy and you haven't got any intention of ....of...loving him back. You scheming little bitch."

The words landed like severe blows to the pit of

Beth's stomach, causing simultaneous pain and panic.

"The bishop is desperate for him to move to the town to develop the centre and use his gifts properly and he won't make a decision. And that's because of you! He thinks poor little you can't survive without him."

Laura paused for breath and saw the tears that were starting to pour down Beth's face.

"Save your waterworks, lady," she said. "They won't work on me. We've all had our problems. All of us. We just put them to one side and get on with things. But not you, you make a career out of your misfortunes, if they can be called misfortunes. Your pneumonia was one, and I've seen the scars on your wrists. It was that pathetic little cry for help that got Matthew trapped in your nasty, sticky web in the first place. But I see right through you."

Laura was savouring every minute of her outburst. It had been planned line by line and had slowly fermented in her head for weeks.

"I know all your tricks. You even got my bloody dog fawning after you. Yes, I know all about that too! You'd have Matthew curled up on the foot of your bed too if you could."

There was triumph in her eyes, and all her

pretence of being a lonely soul just trying to do good and spread the love was gone.

Beth's reaction changed at that instant. Laura was judging her without the first idea of what had changed her life. Laura, the self-appointed epitome of Christian charity and goodness. She had kept her own pain locked away and had not shared her agonies with anyone for fear of reawakening the terrors she had deliberately suppressed.

"How dare you judge me?" Beth demanded.

"Because I know you better than you think," Laura retorted.

Beth stood up but the anger in her face made it cross Laura's mind momentarily that she was going to hit her. She had not expected that, but she was ready, pneumonia or not. She would give as good as she got, she thought.

Beth carefully lifted her shirt and revealed the scars across her midriff. She had never intentionally shown them to anyone before and she was amazed she was doing so now. "SLAG"

Laura saw the scarring carved deeply into her flesh, still red and angry.

"Here's something you don't know about me. You haven't seen these scars, have you, Laura?"

Beth asked. "Should I have just put these to one side too?"

Laura looked away from the sight.

"You can't even look at them," Beth said. "I have to live with them."

Beth knew that Laura was totally taken aback and that her prepared speech no longer had any validity.

"Admit it, Laura, this isn't just about Matthew's vocation. You're scared that I want to keep him to myself, and take him away from you, but I don't. When something like this happens," she nodded at her scars, "you don't think like that."

She sat down slowly. "Laura, I was attacked, raped, mutilated and left for dead. Yes, we all have our problems, but I can't put mine aside as easily as you think, and I certainly don't have the energy to manipulate people with them. It's a struggle every single day to stop myself thinking about it."

Laura was floundering. She had come to say her piece, to get Beth to release her grip on Matthew, and she had found out that everything she had thought about her had been completely wrong. Apologies did not come easily to Laura, especially to someone she had held a grudge against for so long.

Beth continued quietly, "I tried to kill myself and failed, but I meant it. It was no pathetic little cry for help, and when I recovered, I was locked into a nightmare. Matthew has helped me get my life back, little by little."

"I had no idea. He never said," she said miserably.

"He couldn't, could he?"

Laura stood up and prepared to leave. "I've made a fool of myself, and I'm sorry." she said. "I've volunteered to help with the Hargreaves children for a few days, but I'll keep out of your way."

"Did you do that out of your Christian duty, Laura," Beth asked with uncharacteristic bitterness, "or did you do it to impress Matthew?"

Laura did not answer. The words hit home. Beth understood Laura, and she saw things in Laura that the woman didn't want anyone to see. She nodded her head briefly in farewell and left, totally mortified.

Beth was at the lowest she had been since her bad days at The Manor. This time her battle was with the panic inside her that told her she had to let Matthew move on and that she had to cope without him. She did not have a romantic attachment to him, or so she wanted to believe, but she knew she had a dependency that she wasn't sure she could sever. The panic was so bad that, for the first time since leaving the hospital, she took the weightiest dose of Diazepam she was allowed to help get her emotions under control.

She wouldn't let herself be too hard on Laura: the woman couldn't help loving Matthew. She was actually grateful to know that she was the reason he wouldn't make a decision, and why he was so tortured, although she could have done without the vicious verbal assault.

She needed to let him move away but she didn't know if she was strong enough to manage without him, or if she was even strong enough to see the separation through. She really hated that day: she had been living in the bubble of comfortable security that he had helped her create, and now she had to burst that bubble and let him escape, whether she was ready or not.

Chapter Twenty-Four

Matthew called in to check on Beth as soon as he could get round to The Willows. He had had a visit from Laura and was aware that there had been a scene of her making that afternoon. He knew as she spoke that the woman was launching a damage limitation exercise and had been conservative with the truth, so he was full of dread about the effect she had had on Beth.

He knew immediately that it was catastrophic, even allowing for her illness. Her eyes were dull and sore-looking, and she looked even more tiny and shrunken than before.

He sat down beside her and took her hand.

"Laura's been to see me. Whatever has she said?'

Beth was surprised that Laura had faced up to him, but she had no confidence she had told the complete truth.

'She came to tell me that I'm responsible for you not being able to follow your calling," Beth said. It was difficult enough. He did not need to know the personal insults that had been launched at her.

Beth was very clear in what she wanted to achieve. She wanted him to listen to her and take in what she had to say. She had never felt so wretched because, deep down, she knew she wanted him to stay and take care of her as he had always done.

"You can't turn down the bishop's offer just because of me. You know it's what you want to do," she said. "You can't deny yourself what you really want to do just so you're on hand to help me. I won't let you do that for me.'

He picked up the pack of Diazepam that sat near her glass of water. "You're doing so well that you still need these?"

"I had a panic attack after Laura left. She said some very unpleasant things," Beth replied, "but I'm over that now."

He knew that she must have been desperate to have taken any medication because she'd worked so hard to wean herself off it. He realised it must have been quite a scene she'd been through with Laura. He could see she was being diplomatic in not giving the detail. It was obvious she was upset, and he needed her to need him.

"I can't leave you, Beth," he said. "I don't want to put pressure on you to come with me, but I do need you, so I don't want to leave."

It was the first time he had ever acknowledged out loud just how important she had become to him. His words brought tears to her sore eyes and made them sting. She wiped her hand across her face to brush them away.

"And I can't stand in your way." She swallowed hard. "Of course I want you to stay, but not like that, when you know you want to be somewhere else and you're going against your conscience. I'm holding you back. I'm using you as a crutch, and that's not fair. I am better than I was and think I could manage by myself here."

She turned to face him and said the hardest words she had ever spoken, 'I do love you, Matthew, but not in a way that's worth giving up your calling for. You have to stand true to that, and deep down you know it. My love for you is so very needy that it's selfish and that makes it wrong. I'd just take, I can't give anything back. Absolutely nothing."

Of course, she was right, but it didn't make it any easier for him.

"I would give up anything for you," he said. "Anything." He was astonished that today turned into the day when he opened his heart to her. It was so unplanned that he was expressing his feelings badly. It was also such awful timing, she was still so unwell, for him to lay all of this on her. Laura's interference had brought this to pass and there was no going back.

"Are we really saying that walking dogs and watching films and eating pizza together is enough reason for you to turn your back on your calling, because that's all we've got, and it's all I can offer right now?"

"Things might change,' he said. "You might be able to feel different one day."

"Then I'd come straight to you and tell you if it ever happened. And you'd be the only one who could make it happen."

"I'm scared that if I do go, we'd drift apart and you wouldn't let me know if you were struggling, and I'm scared we might lose each other."

She nodded. "You need to think things through

properly," she said. "Don't make me responsible for you losing your vocation, please, Matthew. I promise I will always turn to you. That awful man has done enough damage so please don't let him ruin your life too."

He had so much to think about as he left that he paid scant attention to the PCC meeting he had to attend after he left The Willows. He was surprised to register that the fabric fund was to be boosted by a bingo night and a race night when he read the minutes the next day. He wondered if he'd voted or abstained. He hadn't a clue.

It was becoming clearer that he was going to leave the parish and move to the town. He was going to leave Beth in the village but work out a way to see as much of her as possible. And, most importantly she'd said she loved him, in her own way. He knew there was a limit to that love, but she had actually said it and really meant it. He had never thought she would be able to say those words.

He also hated to admit it, but Laura had actually done him a favour that day. This was painful because, only a couple of hours before, he had been so angry with her he hadn't been able to speak. He had turned his back on her. Now, he had made the decision that had tormented him for so long and he had the hope that one day Beth would come to fully love him.

"What an unexpected relief," he thought to himself as he drifted off to sleep. He wondered how Beth was feeling because she had been so clear and controlled when they parted.

In truth, Beth felt wretched and vulnerable, but she knew that she had done the right thing. She didn't sleep that night. She had reassured him, but she was a long way from convincing herself that she could stand alone.

Chapter Twenty-Five

The village were stunned when the news broke that their popular young vicar was moving on. The elderly ladies were horrified that he was leaving them to face a life that they thought could be fraught with danger. Many of them gave him the benefit of their advice, believing that their age entitled them to tell him what he should do.

He bore all of this with good humour, but he had to work hard to maintain it when they advised him that he should stay and take up with the lovely young nanny he had been seeing. It was hard to smile his way through that, but he never let his feelings show.

The parishioners started planning how to mark

his farewell. There was to be a special lunch on his last Sunday. Parishioners were going to take along food to put out and be shared before the goodbye speeches. A collection had been started to buy him a gift and it was accumulating a significant amount of money. When they asked what he wanted them to buy he told them he wanted them to give it to the centre.

It was noticeable that donations eased off when this became known. That particular initiative did not inspire many of his supporters: if they couldn't persuade him to stay, they'd wanted him to have something nice to remember them with, they said.

Beth was quite apart from all of this planning, but she heard about it as she and the children took their walks to the village and called in at the deli. She was glad that he was well-loved in the parish: he deserved that. She was still fearful of how she would cope when he left, but she was recovering well from her recent illness now and was feeling her stamina return.

They had long conversations about keeping in touch. They would have FaceTime, emails and texting, and he planned on regular visits. They just couldn't quantify these visits until he was settled in.

After her first visit to what was going to be his

new home, Beth was under no illusions that she would ever go alone to visit him. The car park he had to use when he was in his flat doubled as an unofficial public dump and there were old fridges and freezers, doors free-swinging, littering the place. Abandoned, stained mattresses languished against the dilapidated fencing. Carrier bags of refuse were spilling out their contents over the tarmac and an emaciated dog was scavenging in them for food.

He walked her from the car park to see the flat. There were youths hanging out on the corners as they passed, and there was a general air of neglect and decay pervading the streets. There were shut up, shuttered shops, all bearing weary and artless graffiti. This was not a journey she would be prepared to make on her own.

The flat was small and dingy. Its walls were browned from the nicotine of countless previous tenants and the smell hung in the curtains and upholstery. Beth hated the thought of Matthew having to live there.

All she could see was despair and defeat, but Matthew could see endless opportunity. He was so enthusiastic to get started that she kept her reservations to herself.

The centre he was going to develop seemed to

her as run down as the rest of the area, but he was confident it could be brought into vibrant life. She was disconcerted when he introduced her to Stefan, the volunteer he had such faith in, because the man had such a menacing presence. She had a strange sense of foreboding, but she dismissed it because Matthew's flat, the whole area and the centre itself had all had a cumulatively depressing effect on her. She knew Stefan was part of the plans for this new venture and Matthew needed him.

Matthew was going to be affiliated to the local parish and his early visits there had established that there was a small core of determined supporters who had already secured the sponsorship of local businesses in a variety of ways. This convinced him that there was potential but all she could see was the effects of generations of poverty and hard times. She cared enough about him to be glad for him that he had re-found his fervour, but she was true enough to herself to admit that this was an environment in which she would not survive.

What did survive was their tight bond. Honesty had allowed it to move on to a deeper footing and they were closer than ever before. He noticed the little things, like the way she held on to his arm when they walked to the centre, and the way she curled close to him when they watched films together on their last few shared evenings before his departure.

Chapter Twenty-Six

Life with the children had got back to near normal and her strength was returning. The children were so pleased to have her back that they didn't notice that their walks were shorter than before, and that there was less running about.

Tess, though she didn't admit it to Beth, was delighted to have her back. She had made some noises to her husband and her brother that she needed to find someone else, but she hadn't meant it and they knew it.

Beth did notice that Oliver Hargreaves was making his visits shorter than ever. He always called in to see the children when he was in the village, but his interaction with them was cursory and now he barely stayed for a quarter of an hour. It occurred to her that he and Tess never crossed paths on these visits, but she dismissed any thoughts of trouble between them because Tess was going to stay in London much more frequently. She still allowed herself to imagine that their life together was better there.

In truth, Tess started taking advantage of Beth again soon after she appeared to be coping with her work. As her absences became more frequent, and slightly longer, Beth was left alone with the children for increasing amounts of time. Tom Grace came down at the weekends when he could, and he took the children out, allowing her a break. They were visiting animal sanctuaries, soft play centres and activity venues with him, and generally having the fun they should have been having with their parents.

She got on as well as she could with Tom. He was always very appreciative of her work with the children, exasperated by the absences of his sister and aware of her need to have an occasional break from duty.

All of this limited the contact she could have with Matthew. Sundays were never going to be a good day for him with his commitment to his new parish church, but he did manage to extricate himself on Saturdays and come over to the village to see her.

Tongues were wagging amongst the elderly parishioners who noticed his car parked on the Hargreaves' drive each weekend. They had always known that something was going on, they said to each other when they met to catchup on village gossip. It was a pity he hadn't listened to their advice, and then he'd still be with them, they grumbled.

Beth was pleased to see the excitement and enthusiasm in Matthew. She was happy to listen to his updates on the refurbishments going on and the initiatives he had started. He had developed a few of his ideas and strategies when he'd worked there as a volunteer, and now his new role allowed him to develop them. He could see the centre begin to flourish.

One of the things he was particularly pleased with was the food bank that they had established in the back of the building. They were only supplying basic food items and toiletries, but he knew how much they were needed, and the local supermarkets were being reliably supportive.

He was concerned about what he heard from Beth about the Hargreaves' domestic arrangements. He was far from sure that Tess spent her time away from the children with her husband. He had heard a fair amount of gossip about Tess when he had worked in the parish. However, he was not a man to pass on idle talk, so he kept it to himself. He knew it would worry Beth.

He had also heard a few comments about Oliver Hargreaves, which again he kept to himself. There were comments about his overly fastidious grooming, his finely shaped eyebrows and the slightly affected way that he spoke. He was aware of the underlying innuendoes but never responded.

He had heard a few say that he was never seen with his wife or children unless there was a camera about and knew that Beth was well aware of the truth of that. There was no need for discussion.

He knew that Beth only concerned herself with the Hargreaves as parents and she was totally realistic in her assessment of that, though exceedingly tactful in voicing it. He was suspicious of the way the brother, Tom Grace, kept turning up but Beth insisted it was because he was totally besotted by the children. Matthew was not convinced but kept his own counsel, knowing it was verging on jealousy.

He had the uneasy feeling that a storm could break over the Hargreaves marriage at any time. He hoped and prayed he was wrong.

Chapter Twenty-Seven

The storm did break, but not in the way Matthew anticipated. It was much worse.

Tess was in the kitchen with Beth and the children when she received a call. Her words etched themselves in Beth's mind because they were all she had to make sense of the situation.

"You are fucking joking," she said. "This is not funny." There was a long pause whilst she continued listening. The colour drained from her face and her hands started to shake.

"O.K. I'm leaving now," she said, and terminated the call.

"I've got to go," she said to Beth. "I'm going to pack a few things and then I have to leave. Something's happened. I'll keep in touch."

That was exactly how much Beth knew when Tess Hargreaves walked out of her home and left her two children behind.

Beth heard her crashing about upstairs: drawers were being opened and slammed shut, cupboard doors were being banged and expletives were being screamed. Tess struggled downstairs, dragging what was obviously a very heavy case behind her. It kept binding on the bannisters and she had to keep yanking it free.

Beth walked through to the hallway and opened the door for her. Tess snatched her keys from the hall table and left the house, smashing the door-frame with her case as she battled through.

Silently, Beth followed her, aware there was a crisis and trying to be as supportive as she could. She opened the boot of the car and helped Tess haul the case inside. She had never seen her in such a state.

"Look after the children," she said. She got into the car, slammed the door and, without a single glance, reversed straight out of the drive. Beth heard a screech of brakes and a car horn being blasted, then she heard Tess's car accelerate away.

She went back into the kitchen and smiled reassuringly at the children.

"Mummy gone," Harry said solemnly.

"Yes," Beth said evenly, "Mummy's gone."

"Can we go to the park now?" Martha asked, totally unconcerned.

"Yes," Beth said. "I think that's a very good idea. Let's make some sandwiches first, and then we can have a picnic."

The children liked packing up picnics and had grown confident in gathering together bottles of water and fruit whilst Beth made up their sandwiches.

"Cake today?" asked Martha, lifting the tin with their baking in.

"Yoghurt," Beth replied, and the little girl went and got them and put them into the bag with three spoons.

Even though she was stressed by Tess's abrupt departure Beth was still able to enjoy the children's growing independence. Whilst they put their shoes on and collected their coats, she swiftly rearranged the picnic bag without them noticing her corrections. She added the box of sandwiches and carried the bag to the hall..

Boo was turning herself inside out at the sight of the picnic bag, she knew it meant a trip to the park, so Beth slipped her into her harness and clipped on her lead. She had already popped some dog treats into the bag.

It calmed Beth to be restoring a little harmony and normality to what had turned into an odd day. She was beginning to feel like she was back in own their little world, miles away from Tess' troubles, and her spirits lifted. She would text Matthew from the park to update him,

The sun broke through and that encouraged the birds to start singing. The four of them, dog included, had a happy couple of hours. The children enjoyed romping with the dog so much they were too tired for the swings. When they sat down they were totally breathless and had to recover before they could eat their picnic.

"That was good," Harry said, nodding in agreement with himself.

"You've worn Boo out," Beth said.

The dog had curled up in the shade under the tree, close to their blanket. The children always ate without talking when it was a picnic and they'd been chasing about. The food was exactly the same as they would have had at home, but there they would have lingered over it, chatting away. Here they just ate silently, ravenously hungry after all their exercise.

It was one of their best outings and they were a happy little group as they decided to head home. Both children said they were worn out, and Beth was not going to argue if they wanted to go straight for a nap.

Matthew texted her as they were about to leave. His message was to the point.

"Check out the news on your phone. I'm on my way over."

The news headlines stunned her. Oliver and an unnamed man had been taken by ambulance into hospital. The man had died on the journey and Oliver was said to be in a coma. The police were treating the flat as a crime scene and had sealed it off.

She tried to act naturally as she packed up their things and walked them back home. She could not believe the sight that greeted them as the house came into view. The place was swarming with journalists and photographers. Two television crews were setting up. For a minute she was unsure what to do, but then she found some courage.

"Come on," she took hold of their little hands, put her head down and made for the gate. Her heart was pounding and the old panic was trying to engulf her as she barged her way through.

"Excuse me," she said, her voice unusually loud and confident. "Children coming through."

She had calculated that the press would let two little children through no matter what story they were after. She was right but had not anticipated the barrage of questions that were fired at her. The shouts jumbled together, but she made out a couple.

"Is Tess Hargreaves home?"

"How is Oliver Hargreaves?"

She made no answer as she tried to get them into the house. Her hands were shaking, and she found herself fumbling with the lock. She shut the door, pulled the bolts across and sighed with relief.

Children first, she told herself as she decided what to do. She released the fretful dog from her harness then took them upstairs and put the television on for them.

"What are those people here for?" Martha asked. "They wanted Mummy."

"Oh, I think they just wanted to take some more pictures of you two with Mummy, like they did before," she said, deflecting their concern. She kept her voice as light as possible whilst she got them to settle on the settee. "No photos until you two have had a rest and got some clean clothes on. You're a pair of scruffs."

She couldn't wait to get downstairs and make it more secure. The press were crowding around the house, peering through windows and flashes were bouncing in as they pressed their phones and cameras against the windows in the hope of capturing a scoop picture. They were ringing the doorbell incessantly and calling the home number.

She ran around to close the curtains and pull down the blinds. She unplugged the home phone and disconnected the doorbell. All she could think of doing was to press the panic button on the alarm system and report directly to the police station that the house was under siege and that she was alone with the children.

"Beff," she heard Harry call.

She turned and saw two frightened little children at the top of the stairs.

"We don't like it," Martha said.

Beth ran upstairs and hugged the two scared little mites. "Come on, let's watch TV together," she said. "We can have a cuddle." She turned the TV to the Disney Channel and, for the very first time, was glad to have the TV to keep the children entertained.

She double checked her phone. There was still no word from Tess.

Chapter Twenty-Eight

As the children settled in close to her and started to watch their film Beth had the chance to check her phone for news updates. She learned the police were treating the flat as a crime scene and that Oliver Hargreaves was in a critical condition.

Beth read the headlines over and over. She was totally overwhelmed; the shock of the news made her shake and she desperately fought to control her rising panic. At that point she was assuming that Tess had fled to her husband's bedside and that there had been a murder attempt. It was all too close to what she had been through and she was scared of the wave of feeling that was engulfing her.

She texted Matthew. "Where are you? Text when you get here and I'll let you in."

"Five minutes," came the reply. She registered he shouldn't be texting when he was driving but was relieved he was close.

"The police are going to come round," she said to the children. "The nosey people outside are being very rude to us by banging on our door and our windows and shouting through the letterbox."

"Will they make them go away?" Martha asked.

"I'm sure they will," Beth said, and she hugged them both more tightly.

After a few minutes she remembered that she still had Tom Grace's number in her phone. She texted him, "Tess has packed some things and gone, and the children and I are trapped in the house under siege from the press. Please help." She had thought about calling him but was concerned that the children would be frightened by what she said.

He texted back immediately. "I'm on my way. Two hours at best."

At last she had a text from Matthew to say he was at the door.

She ran down to open it, and there was barging and scuffling from outside as he squeezed through the throng of journalists. He then had to exert his entire body weight against the door to close it against the pressure they were exerting. He fastened the locks and bolts as fast as he could.

"Come upstairs," she said. "The children are terrified."

Chapter Twenty-Nine

The police were helpful and arrived quickly. They restored some order amongst the waiting journalists and so they were no longer near to the windows and doors.

The most senior policeman consulted with them and advised that a brief press statement be made in the hope they would see they were wasting their time. Together they drafted a few sentences that they hoped would pacify them.

"Mrs Hargreaves will be away from home for the fore-seeable future. The only occupants of the house are two very frightened children and their nanny. They cannot help you with your questions.

In the interests of the children's well-being, please respect their privacy at this difficult time and stay outside the gates.

No information will be released from this house and no one will be returning to offer you any new information.

The police ask you to support us and to comply with this request.

Thank you all."

Matthew agreed to read it. When he had finished, questions were shouted but he made no attempt to answer them. He folded his script and went back inside, breathing a sigh of relief as he closed the door behind him that this time there was no pushing.

"When I woke up this morning I didn't expect to find myself on the six o'clock news," he said.

"Are you going to be on the television?" Martha asked. "Can we watch?"

That was the last thing that Beth and Matthew wished them to see so neither answered the question. They all watched from the playroom window to see what would happen. It was clear that the journalists were phoning their editors and Beth took all the head nodding as a good sign. Some journalists gathered in groups to talk things over, and though they couldn't second-guess what they would eventually decide to do, they were thrilled to see one of the television cameras being packed away.

"When will we have some dinner?" Harry

asked. He was sitting on the floor, playing with a chunky plastic aeroplane.

Everyone in the room laughed with relief. The little boy had become totally absorbed in play and was now more concerned about his hunger than the hubbub outside.

Whilst the most senior of the policemen went outside to talk to the remaining journalists to find out their intentions, Beth set about getting a meal ready. Tess was still not answering her phone so they knew they couldn't make any decisions until Tom Grace appeared.

"Some of them are going," the policeman reported. "They've been ordered back to London, but a few will hang on. We'll stay on for a while to make sure that everything settles, then I'll leave someone posted to keep an eye on things."

Beth felt slightly reassured when she heard there would be a policeman outside. She was fighting to control the old feelings that kept erupting inside her and she badly wanted some time alone with Matthew, but the children remained her priority. She concentrated on cooking their pasta.

She still only knew what her quick internet searches had revealed and her head was reeling with shock. Matthew hadn't been able to find anything else out.

The children had an early night and they made no protest. They were exhausted and dark-eyed by then and ready to sleep. They kept to the usual routine and it was only after she had closed their door that she allowed the tears to pour down her face. Matthew took one look at her and opened his arms and she melted into his hug with the greatest sense of relief. She had never been in his arms before, but that didn't occur to either of them. It was just a matter of comfort.

Eventually they sat down together, Beth curled against him, and they flicked through the TV menu to find the latest updates. It was dominating all the news channels. The body had been identified as that of a fifteen-year-old youth, Oliver Hargreaves was still in a coma and police were waiting to interview him. There was no sign of Tess Hargreaves, and it was reported that she had left her home but her whereabouts were now unknown. There was footage of the press outside The Willows, and Matthew's statement was replayed.

The news channel repeated those known details interminably, and the ticker tape headlines across the bottom of the screen echoed the same messages over and over.

"This is a waste of time," he said, and turned the TV off.

He had a much closer grasp on what was going on than Beth, who had suspected nothing of Oliver Hargreaves' secret life. Beth's brain had assumed that it had been an attack, probably because of what she'd been through.

She hadn't suspected his homosexuality previously because, for the sake of the children, she had managed to cast him and keep him in the role of a distant but high-achieving father.

"Maybe he thought he could keep it quiet if he operated in the shadows," Matthew suggested to her.

"But that could open him up to blackmail," Beth countered. "Perhaps that's what's behind it."

"I don't think we can guess what was going on last night," he said, " but I'm sorry it's come out of the blue for you."

He pulled her closer. "How are you doing?" he asked.

"The truth? Badly. I feel as if a lot of old feelings are coming back," she said.

He expected that. An incident like this,

involving someone she knew, was always going to hit hard and jolt her memories awake. What he didn't know was how to help her and protect her.

He was glad they had come closer of late and he was able to hold her to give her comfort, unlike when they had first met. In those days he'd have never have got through her self-protective no-go zone.

Tom Grace's arrival brought no clarification as he explained that Tess had not contacted him and was not answering either her phone or messages. The police would not give him any information and the hospital would not discuss Oliver Hargreaves, even with him, his brother-in-law.

He had formulated clear plans on his drive over. He had decided to take control of the children's welfare. He planned to take Beth and the children up to his home in Bradford to get them away from the media circus and get the children into some sort of normality.

He was incandescent with rage at both his sister and his brother-in-law. He was so angry he could not, at that moment, explain himself adequately.

He knew what had to be done, and that was his entire focus. He issued this as a take-it-or-leave-it statement to Beth. She was stunned by his attitude.

Matthew was not sure how Beth would cope being taken away from the security and familiarity of the village when she was so emotional, and he didn't want her far away from him and his protection. He voiced his objections without referencing Beth's personal issues.

Beth was grateful. She did not want to be forced into a completely different environment with the children. She was scared of urban life, and she was scared about being trapped indoors with the children in a strange house. She was also terrified of a separation from Matthew. She told Tom she wasn't sure she could go with them.

The strange thing was that Tom, usually so affable and reasonable where Beth was concerned, didn't care if she went or not.

"The children are coming with me," he said. "I really want you to come too, Beth. I know how important you are to them, but I'll take them on my own if I have to."

It seemed both strange and extreme to Beth and Matthew. They could see the press presence made it very awkward for the children, but it was now much calmer and more controlled. They were no longer besieging the house and were waiting patiently on the pavement.

As far as Tom saw it, this had nothing at all to do with the priest. His only concern was to get the children away from this circus and under his protection. He made it difficult for himself by not offering any reasoning, and Beth felt stressed by his non-negotiable decision.

He knew he really needed her with them, but such was his determination, such was his level of stress, that he was prepared to do all of this without her. At that moment he couldn't summon the effort to entreat or persuade.

"I'm not getting Martha and Harry up now," Beth said firmly. "They've had a very bad day and they need their sleep."

Tom could see the sense in that, and he didn't particularly want to drive back to Bradford that night, possibly pursued by journalists thinking he was taking them to their mother. They were all exhausted, and all three of them knew that the best thing was to try to get some sleep and make the move in the morning.

Matthew saw the panic in Beth's eyes.

"I'll stay," he said.

Tom looked at him in astonishment. What was it, he wondered, with this priest? What had his niece and nephew got to do with him? Why did he need to be constantly hovering over the nanny?

"All this has upset Beth, and I don't want her on her own tonight. She's only just got over pneumonia."

Matthew, unlike Tom, was aware that Beth was on the precipice of a relapse into her former traumatised state and he wasn't going to let it happen or discuss it. There was a couch in the large nursery, and that was where he was going to spend the night, whether Tom Grace liked it or not. It never occurred to him to check with Beth.

He didn't need to. She was overwhelmed with gratitude.

Chapter Thirty

Beth woke early the next morning. A quick check through the curtains revealed that the press were still camped outside, though fewer in number. The children were fast asleep.

They had been too tired to talk the previous night, though neither had found it easy to drift off to sleep, so they had a lot to discuss that morning. Beth slipped her dressing gown on and went to join Matthew in the nursery. He was already dressed and was busy folding up his blankets.

They settled to talk, and Beth was searingly honest. She wanted to be with the children but the thought of looking after them in a strange city made her feel panic rising and her breath shortening.

Matthew admitted that he couldn't take time off from the centre no matter how much he wanted to support her, but he also said he could see no reason why Tom Grace was so insistent on such a move for the children. He knew he cared a lot for them, but to be prepared to uproot them and separate them from Beth seemed totally out of character and cruel in these circumstances.

They checked the TV for news and found there had been some updates. The body had been identified as a runaway who had been working as a rent boy in the capital for some months. It had been established that his death, and Oliver Hargreaves' coma, had been caused by the side effects of taking an adulterated dose of cocaine.

Oliver Hargreaves was said to have regained consciousness and the police were waiting until the doctors allowed them to interview him. The Prime Minister had issued a statement expressing shock and had dismissed Oliver from his post with immediate effect. The constituency Conservative Party had announced that it would be meeting later that day to discuss their course of action.

The updates came as hammer blows. It seemed impossible that the man that they had known had fallen from grace so spectacularly and it seemed tragic that the children would have to live from then on with a shadow over their name. It made them realise how superficial their knowledge of him had been.

"Poor Tess," Beth said, sighing from deep within her chest. Her feelings were so churned up that it was hard to keep her composure.

"Beth, Tess has walked out on you and her children. She may have gone into hiding, but she's clearly not thinking about them. That is a statement of fact, not a judgment," he said.

She knew that he was right.

She checked the children: they were both still fast asleep, but she could hear Tom Grace moving about downstairs. Matthew went down to join him whilst Beth pulled on her clothes. She joined them, anxious about what Tom would do next.

He had made coffee, but he looked as if he had not slept at all. They sat round the big old table together and he apologised for his abruptness the previous day. He seemed more like the man they had previously known, but heavily burdened in a way he needed to explain.

He said he had to tell them his story, but that it was very difficult for him because it compromised

Tess, Oliver and the children, and he'd vowed to keep it hidden.

It was incredible to Beth and Matthew that things could become even more complex, but it appeared that that was just what was about to happen. His story was long and complex and they listened in astonishment.

Chapter Thirty-One

Tom's story added to the shock and confusion they were feeling. He explained that Tess was his adopted sister, having joined his family at the age of eight. At seventeen she had left her adopted home without a word and had gone to London to pursue a career in advertising. Even at that age she had all the confidence of someone who had become used to life entirely on her own terms. She never contacted her adoptive parents again and all their efforts to trace her failed.

The first thing they heard, years after her disappearance, was her marriage to a newly-elected Conservative MP, the son of a knighted industrialist and the product of a privileged background and education. They saw it in the national press and were astonished that the person they had filed as missing, the person they had looked for for years, had suddenly appeared in bridal photographs in the society pages.

The hurt was immense, yet they did not try to make contact with her from then on. She was clearly well-positioned and in no danger, and obviously had no intention of renewing their relationship. She had ignored all of their previous attempts to trace her so was unlikely to welcome fresh ones. They were decent people who finally accepted that she had no place in her life for them, so they hid their pain and carried on.

Tom had heard nothing from her either, and then, two years after her wedding, she tracked him down through his company's website. She had asked to meet, and they got together in London in a bistro of her choosing.

She appeared distraught. She explained that she and her husband were encountering infertility problems and she wanted his help. Through tears, she told him that her husband's sperm count was so low that he had no chance of fathering a child and, for other reasons too, they had been advised that IVF with donor sperm was the only way forward. She explained, becoming more and more emotional, that she was under pressure from the Hargreaves dynasty to produce an heir, and that under no circumstances were they to discover Oliver's problem.

In short, she was asking Tom to become a sperm donor.

He explained his shock, his initial horror and repulsion at the idea of fathering the child of the girl who had grown up alongside him as his younger sister. He was also angry at the way she could meet him after all this time without asking after their parents. He also doubted Tess had any maternal instincts, though he could see her dynastic ambitions clearly.

Her approaches became relentless and even more emotional and, in a moment of weakness, after a lengthy barrage of messages and phone calls begging, pleading and hinting at self-harm, he had agreed, despite all his anger and misgivings. The truth was that she had worn him down and he could no longer say no.

She had arranged a private clinic for the treatment and had not been there on the day he visited. That was it. He had succumbed and, as always, she had got her own way.

What he didn't know, and what she had deliberately not bothered to tell him, was that other fertilised embryos had been stored and, unknowingly, he was to become Harry's father as well.

Whilst Tess had not kept in touch with him, he had seen Martha's birth announcement in the society pages and realised that he had successfully fathered her child. He was stunned to hear of the arrival of Harry so quickly afterwards, and he suspected he might be his father too.

He had been tormented by the knowledge that he had fathered two children and the fear that Tess was unlikely to be a natural and nurturing mother led him, against all his reasoning, to make contact. He had no wish to reunite with Tess, but the children were his priority.

He had made himself a regular visitor, almost forcing himself into their family life. Tess, aware that he alone knew their secret, was, for once, too scared to push for her own way and deny him access. He had become Uncle Tom, a regular visitor and his presence hovered over her threateningly and over the children protectively. He ensured that they received affection and fun from him. She was acutely aware she was being monitored. He always knew they would come to no harm with her, but he was never confident they were loved and cared for as they should have been.

Beth and Matthew were amazed. The situation was so complex and now they started to see things with much greater clarity.

"Did she know about Oliver?" asked Beth.

"She knew right from the start," he said. "She told me so. She married him for his money and his family connections, but I think he would have been the donor for the children if he had been able."

"So their whole life was a sham," Beth said, realisation dawning about the plight of the two little ones who had been so wanted but so uncared for.

They sat in silence, drinking their coffee. They knew now why Tom Grace was so strongly attached to the children. Eventually he started to speak again. He tried to explain his plans, as far as he had reasoned them out.

He needed to get paternity tests done rapidly to establish that he was their biological father and he was going to consult a solicitor about how to get a residency order and obtain parental responsibility. He wanted to act quickly to keep out intervention by the Hargreaves dynasty, who had no history of emotional connection with the children but would most likely want them to secure the family businesses into the future. Again, people with no real interest in Martha or Harry.

To do all this he planned to move them back to his home in Bradford: Tess knew where his business was based, but that was in Leeds and she didn't know his home address. He knew that no one in the office would ever divulge it.

The extent of his plans astounded both Beth and Matthew, but as they sat and considered what he said, the tragic reality dawned that what he proposed was possibly the very best outcome the two children could have. Their father was disgraced and faced a certain jail sentence and their mother, never the most caring of parents, had abandoned them a second time, this time in the middle of a major crisis and was neither answering calls or texts.

"I'll come with you," Beth said suddenly. "The children love you and they should be with you. You're the only one I've ever seen show any real concern for them."

Matthew was astonished at her newly found determination, but he could see she was resolute. He understood her motivation. He had previously suspected that Tom Grace was interested in Beth for herself, but now he could see that Beth had been right all along. She was only important to him as the children's carer. He would have supported her whatever she decided, now he had to help make her move to Bradford as smooth as he could.

"We could load up my car with some fo the things they'll need, and I'll drive Beth up for you, but I can't stay. Do you want me to look after the dog?"

"No, they'll need Boo to provide a bit of familiarity at my house," he said, "and here they are now! Good morning little terrors." The two appeared, pyjama-clad and dishevelled at the kitchen door.

"How would you like to come to my house for a holiday?"

"With Beff?" asked Harry, "And Boo?"

Tom nodded.

"We'll come then," announced Martha.

It was settled as quickly as that, underlining to them all that the children were perfectly happy with Tom and Beth, and that they were not at all concerned about their missing parents.

Chapter Thirty-Two

Matthew reversed his car into the empty garage and closed the heavy doors. They were able to load up his car through the back door of the garage, far away from the eyes of the press.

It took a surprisingly long time to assemble what the children and Beth would need. Beth, ever practical, tried to anticipate every possible eventuality. She realised that a single man would be unlikely to have the towels and linen they would need for their stay, and totally unlikely to have food supplies to tide them over, even for a few days. She even had the dog's needs to cater for.

Both men realised that all that was required of them was to carry boxes and pack the cars and keep the children entertained. They were astonished at just how much was needed for a smooth transfer if the children were to regard this as a holiday and not an emergency evacuation.

The children set about choosing their toys, and Beth packed them, replacing some of their random selections with trusted favourites. She smiled to herself as she did this, some of their choices had been so obscure. Why would any child choose a plastic spatula as an essential toy? It reminded her just how young and vulnerable the two of them were.

Beth was not prepared to drive the Corsa to Bradford. She was perfectly happy to shuttle the children to and from their swimming lessons in it and to make the local journeys they needed, but the thought of motorway driving, with all this on her mind, was beyond her. She also knew she would never dare drive it in a strange city.

At last the cars were loaded. Tom had child seats in his car already, so all he had to do was supply the post code for Matthew's Satnav and load the dog and children into his car. His car was still on the drive so this aroused the press's curiosity. Their worst fear was that they would do a paparazzi-style tailing operation, thinking the children were being taken to visit their parents. The press had still not tracked Tess Hargreaves' location and her story was their ultimate goal.

They decided that Matthew should speak to the journalists that remained, and that Tom should keep out of the picture completely. There was just one policeman in attendance now, so he was consulted quickly before Matthew gave their statement to the press.

There were no longer TV crews outside, and the numbers were reduced, so he just went over to them to explain it all in a chat. He told them that the children had to be protected from all of the interest and so they were being taken on a brief holiday. He assured them, and stressed to them, that no one within the house had received news on, or from, either Tess or Oliver Hargreaves.

With that, he opened the big gates to allow the cars to leave and asked the press not to invade the garden again to try for pictures through the windows as they drove off. He found them amenable: one of the journalists even offered to close the gates after them.

Their departure went smoothly. They set the alarm, having informed the voice on the other end that the house would now remain unoccupied for the foreseeable future. Martha and Harry scrambled into Tom's car with all the eagerness of young adventurers off on holiday, and Boo ambled up to join them. They waved happily to the press as they drove off whilst the adults tried to keep their faces turned away.

It was good for Beth and Matthew to make the drive together. They were able to talk things over openly. Both had a head full of fears and concerns. They were convinced of one thing, that Tess would construe their actions as a betrayal. They could imagine her claiming they'd aided an abduction. However, they were now sure it was the very best course of action for the children and they told each other had no need to examine their consciences further.

Both were concerned about the likely length of the stay in Bradford. Beth had no wish to relocate there permanently. Neither of them had any idea what Tom's long-term decisions would be if his attempts to gain parental rights were successful. They had no way of knowing how long all of this would take.

The house in Bradford was a detached house, typical of the double fronted, bay-windowed type built all over the country in the 1930s. The previous owners had preserved the integrity of the exterior but had remodelled inside extremely successfully.

Beth was relieved that there were three bedrooms, she had half expected to be sleeping on a sofa in the children's room. Tom Grace's room had an en-suite, so she and the children had full use of the family bathroom and the other two bedrooms, and so the whole thing seemed manageable and she felt more at ease.

Harry and Martha explored the house and gardens, accompanied by a curious dog who needed to sniff out her new territory with diligent thoroughness.

The adults unloaded the cars and hauled their contents into vaguely the correct rooms. Within half an hour the immaculate, minimalist interior was cluttered with bags and boxes, but no one cared about that. They had done what they intended, and the children were safe and protected from the eyes of the press.

They made coffee and sat together in the kitchen area and all expressed relief that the transfer was over. The children were perfectly content and were unlikely to be discovered there and Tess could not find them.

The shock of Tom's revelations still hung heavily in the air, each one of them uncertain where his chosen path for the children would lead.

Chapter Thirty-Three

It proved relatively easy to settle into a routine. Things were unpacked and stowed away without difficulty because Tom had accumulated so little clutter. There were plenty of empty cupboards and drawers to accommodate their things.

The children adjusted to life in the downstairs open plan area very quickly. Beth was able to take them for walks to the local park and to the nearby shops and kept them to their routine of activities and naps as much as possible. That was as much as she felt able to do in the strangeness of the outside world, but she ran the house with her usual care.

The paternity tests arrived on their first full day in Bradford and she swabbed their little mouths, explaining that Uncle Tom just wanted to be sure everything was ok. The three of them walked to the post box with the pre-paid envelopes that morning, the children little realising the implications of the envelopes they had just squabbled over as they both had wanted to put them through the slot. They did one each and peace was restored.

Tom and Beth continued diligently to contact Tess several times a day, but the messages went unanswered and the phone went directly to voice-mail. They did not have a clue where she was, and the TV news surmised that she had gone into hiding as nothing had been seen of her at the hospital.

They would have been more worried if she hadn't regularly re-recorded her voicemail message. The changes increased the drama behind the message but were reassuring to Tom and Beth. It went from "I can't take your call" to "I can't possibly take your call" to "There's no way I can get back to you at present".

Tom, a graphic designer, had had an attic conversion so that he could work from home when he pleased, and he started to stay home every day. He had many calls to make to his solicitor and he needed privacy to do that. His staff were a loyal crew and he knew they would not divulge his address at any price, but he still didn't want them overhearing his conversations and speculating over them.

He had decided he would not contact Social Services, though he knew he would have to eventually. He would wait until the results of the paternity tests had come through. They took three days to arrive, but when they did arrive, they confirmed that he was the father of both children. Beth and Tom were relieved to have that confirmation. It somehow legitimised their actions, and both had harboured secret, unspoken doubts because of Tess's general unreliability.

Beth was terrified about the involvement of Social Services because of her history of mental illness, but the solicitor had said it was essential in view of Tom's decisions. The residency orders of the past had been replaced by the Child Arrangements Order, and Tom needed to obtain one. If the court awarded it he would automatically be granted parental responsibility. The courts expected attempts at mediation to be made, but, as Tom had explained to his solicitor, Tess was deliberately keeping herself out of reach and Oliver was in hospital.

The prospect of the visits of the social worker

became more alarming to Beth, who had an over-whelming dread of the children being dragged away and either put into care or taken to their paternal grandparents. She had many nightmares in which the children were pulled forcibly from her arms and she would wake up stricken with terror and soaked in sweat.

Beth's lack of confidence was uncalled for. The uncontrived but harmonious domestic scenes that were witnessed consistently were totally reassuring to the experienced eye of the mature woman who made the visits.

Social Services had chosen their most senior social worker but this case was even outside her experience, despite her lengthy service. Oliver Hargreaves was now such a high-profile national figure, still in hospital but facing serious charges, that there was bound to be press scrutiny. She had to exercise over-zealous diligence for fear of reper-cussions.

Tom provided her with Tess's number so that she could try to get in touch with her. It was hard to believe that Tess ignored the calls from her, even though the voice messages made it absolutely clear a court would be deciding the future of her chil-dren. Both Beth and Tom hoped that that would work in his favour because neither had any faith that Tess would ever change her attitude to the children, no matter what she might say if she bothered to respond.

The social worker was amused by the articulate and consistent way that the children responded to her questions whenever she interviewed them alone. She could see how genuine their affection was for their uncle and their nanny, and how they accepted indifference from both parents as the norm. She could see no reason to doubt that they were in the best possible place, and agreed that they were better there, away from the media circus camped outside their home.

This was all very reassuring to Tom and Beth. Beth now felt thoroughly vindicated in backing Tom, though she was still uneasy about doing it all behind Tess's back. Matthew, speaking on the phone, reassured her that it was hardly behind her back, when she, Tom and Social Services were trying to contact her every day.

Beth spoke daily with Matthew and each week he kept one day clear of commitments so that he could drive over and spend time with her and the children. He was relieved at the way Beth had coped. She was just as she had always been with the children, although ill-at-ease in her wider new surroundings. He understood that the Social Services' endorsement of the arrangements had helped to keep her calm but that she felt out of her depth as soon as she left the house.

Beth was always glad to see him, to have someone to give her a reassuring hug. She had come such a long way since her days in The Manor and she now needed that physical closeness and reassurance. Her exclusion zone was relaxed where Matthew was concerned. She knew it was only he and the children who could enter that invisibly defined area, but she also knew that this was progress: it was more than she had ever dared hope for in those dark old days.

Tom was unaware of all of this, but it never raised itself as an issue because he saw her as the children's nanny and instinctively respected the boundaries that she imposed in her quiet way. She would spend time with him when the children were with them but always retreated to her room rather than be alone with him.

He had no idea how long Beth would want to

stay with his little family unit. He could see her attachment to Matthew, and he had known how the priest felt about her since that night in the hospital. That troubled him because keeping Beth as nanny was instrumental to the wellbeing of his two children. He enjoyed being able to say that, if only to himself.

His children.

He even allowed himself the luxury of thinking that one day he would change their name to Grace. Would they ever call him Daddy, he pondered?

Chapter Thirty-Four

Things took a surprise turn for everyone by a rapid decision made by the Hargreaves dynasty. Their empire of industrial enterprises had always been destined to be Oliver's inheritance, and, ultimately, Harry's. The Hargreaves' world was misogynistic, and they apologised to no one for their attitude and their way of inheritance planning.

Social Services had been in touch with them to update them on the children's situation and to see if they would seek custody of them. Their reaction was immediate. As the paternity test had established Tom was their father, the children were now officially nothing to do with them and they had no familial responsibilities whatsoever. They stated they would not be taking any interest in the court proceedings. They were emphatic that any entitlement the children had had to their estate was severed from that point onwards.

When the news was relayed back to Tom he immediately updated Beth. Both were relieved that they had stepped out of the picture completely but were stunned by their cold and immediate rejection. They realised it was hard for them to comprehend what that family was going through as they faced the forthcoming prosecution of their eldest son. Even so, it seemed brutal for them to totally reject the two children they had thought, up to that point, were their grandchildren.

Charges had not yet been finalised against Oliver, but he was now in custody after his release from hospital. The Hargreaves were under no illusion that they would be serious. They had acted to distance themselves from him immediately, turning their inheritance plans in the direction of their second son. They not only wanted to distance themselves from Oliver, but from anyone connected with Oliver.

It was incomprehensible to Beth that they could act so swiftly to cut the children out of their lives completely. They were so young and they were completely blameless.

Beth remembered the odd times when Tess and Oliver had received orders to take them to visit their grandparents. They had never looked forward to it at all, and neither had the children. In fact, Martha had always declared in vain she wasn't going at all and would be staying with Beth.

Beth had had to dress them in their best and most formal outfits, so they looked uncomfortable and old fashioned, almost Edwardian. She had to groom them as if they were prize exhibits in a show and all she could do for them then was to hug them goodbye. She always hugged them again, consolingly, when they returned and told her that it had all been very horrible.

It made things easier, legally speaking, that the Hargreaves had declared they had no further interest in Martha and Harry. Oliver Hargreaves was facing a lengthy prison sentence, whatever charges were brought, and would be on the sex offenders' register and could never apply for their custody. Tess remained wilfully out of contact and had not responded to Social Services' pleas to attend mediation, so she had ruled herself out of the picture.

There was no point in telling the children about their grandparents' decision as it was totally irrelevant to them. They didn't even like the stern elderly couple and had no comprehension of inheritance. They were not missing their parents either: their happy little world revolved around Uncle Tom, Beth and Boo, as it had done for as long as they wanted to remember. They had shut out the memories of the stream of uncaring nannies months ago.

Neither Beth nor Tom were in any way worried about Tess Hargreaves' safety or whereabouts as they noted, when they tried to call her, she was still changing her voicemail recording regularly, now casting herself in her greetings as a tragic heroine under intense pressure. "I can't possibly speak to anyone" was her latest voicemail greeting.

It was with all this in mind that Tom Grace started to reconsider the way he thought about Beth. It became increasingly apparent that life would be so much more assured and stable for them all if she could be made a permanent part of the family and, as an employee, she could disappear at will. As he mulled this over, he thought about her relationship with Matthew.

He was certain they were not lovers, but he knew they were close. It was all a bit of a mystery to him, because he knew how besotted Matthew was with her. He wondered if their strange relationship had any connection to the hideous scarring that he had seen on Beth that evening when she took ill. He was not a callous man, but he could be calculating, and he was coming to terms with a new world order and was trying to make it the best he possibly could for his children. Those two words again: his children.

He really liked Beth, even though she was always distant when the children weren't around. He admired her quiet efficiency, her affectionate but appropriate ways of dealing with the children and the way she looked after all of them. Unasked, she had supplied him with meals since their arrival in Bradford and taken over the household's laundry.

He decided, on reflection, that making Beth a permanent part of their household would be a very sound way of proceeding. He was not in a relationship and had not been for a couple of years. What encounters he had had in that time had been brief and unsatisfactory.

He could not stand high-maintenance, self-obsessed women and they were the only type to enter his orbit in the time since he had been single. Beth scored highly in this respect: she was not beautiful by any means, but she had a wholesome radiance about her that he had seen slowly develop over the time he had known her.

And so the final part of his strategy fell into place. After he had gained the court's permission to keep the children he would work towards marriage with Beth. He thought no one could be a better mother for his children than the shy nanny who cared for them all so well.

Beth had no idea that all this was in his mind so, when he asked her about staying on permanently in Bradford, she was taken aback. She had understood this to be an emergency and temporary measure only.

She was too honest, too transparent, to dissemble.

"I couldn't live here," she said, "not in the long term. If that is your plan for the children, you need to find someone else." Her heart pounded in panic as she said it because she could not imagine life without Martha and Harry.

It hurt her to say she could not make her life there, but it was true. She was making the best of a difficult situation and was just about coping with the very near neighbourhood and its little row of shops. She had not ventured further, and she knew she couldn't see herself ever doing so. She was feeling confined and missed the village, with its leisurely pace, fresh air and open views. She missed the contact she had with the few people she knew and trusted, and she missed being near to Matthew.

Her words came as a shock to Tom, who had no idea of the limitations her slow recovery imposed on her ability to adapt to a new and busy environment. He assumed it was her desire to be nearer the priest, and he determined to make sure that, from then on, she couldn't take her time off when he visited. He imagined the presence of the children would restrict their conversations and intimacy.

He realised that he had been taking her for granted when he heard her next observations.

"I think the tenancy on The Willows may be at risk. I haven't been paid since the news broke, so I think it's possible the rent hasn't been paid either."

"Why on earth didn't you say you've not been paid?" he asked.

"I was going to, eventually, but it didn't seem that important with all that you've had on your mind.'

He arched his neck backwards and sighed heavily, looking at the ceiling for a while. More things to think about, he told himself inwardly. The Willows suddenly became part of his list of things to sort out.

As he considered it all, moving the family back there once things had settled down might allow Beth to stay on with them until he could persuade her to marry him. It definitely required further thought.

Chapter Thirty-Five

The weeks slipped by and the court hearings moved close. Beth could see things were looking very positive for Tom Grace as everything had gradually fallen into place. Tess had still not replied to any contact from Social Services.

On the day of the hearing he dressed in his business suit, took his folder of documents from his desk and stepped out to discover if his dreams of having his own family would finally materialise. Both he and Beth were in a state of intense anxiety

Beth, unaware of any other dreams he harboured, had supported him wholeheartedly since they'd left the village. She was further reassured because he had demonstrated each day, without any pretence, that he was totally genuine in his desire to keep the children and provide them with the love they needed.

Her brain told her that he would obtain the court order, but her natural wariness made her scared as she watched him drive away. She wondered if Tess would put in a dramatic, last-minute appearance.

If it all worked out, she wondered if the day would come when the children called him Daddy, but she pushed that aside abruptly. It wasn't the title or label that mattered, it was the affection and their bonds that mattered. There had been very little affection provided by the Hargreaves.

Even though she was expecting it, the sound of her phone ringing made her jump and her heart pound. She knew at once he had been successful by the excited tone in his voice. She phoned Matthew immediately to pass on the news. He was pleased that this brought stability to the children but caused him concern over Beth.

"Does that mean you're staying in Bradford?" he asked, filled with fear that the arrangement might become permanent.

"No," she said, "I've already told him that he will need to find someone else if he stays on here. I can't make a life for myself here. I'm living in low-level panic and it's not getting any easier."

He was astonished that she had been so decisive and forthright. He had never broached the issue before because he had been sure that her innate loyalty and diligence would force her stay on, no matter what impact it was having on her. It seemed it was worse for her in Bradford than he had suspected.

"I can't believe you've done that," he said truthfully. "That is amazing."

He meant this as praise because she had been so timid previously in her decision making and so anxious to do what was right for everyone else. His heart also leapt as he wondered if this meant she wanted to return to be near him.

"I know," she agreed. "I was surprised that I was so sure. You know how much I love the children, but I can't live here much longer. Sometimes I feel so anxious it's a struggle to breathe."

"A good day all round, then," he said. "You're making decisions for yourself and the children get a caring father at last."

Tom was home by lunch time and they all sat together round the table to eat.

"I've got some news for you," he said to Martha

and Harry. "You're both going to live with me from now on and I'm going to look after you."

They looked at him with curiosity.

"So this isn't just a holiday?" Martha asked. "It's for ever?"

He nodded, "For ever."

Harry looked up from his plate with troubled eyes. "Beff looks after me for ever," he said shakily.

Beth felt a stab to her heart at the little boy's love for her and she waited anxiously for Tom's reply.

"I'm going to try to make sure Beth looks after you both for a long, long time," he said with such confidence that Beth was stunned. She had told him so clearly that she couldn't make her life in Bradford.

It wasn't the time for her to contradict: that could unsettle them, so she said nothing, and they continued to eat their lunch. Tom noticed with satisfaction that the children were perfectly happy with the new arrangements. Beth, he thought, was another matter, and he was just starting to think that taking over the tenancy of The Willows might be the best solution for them all.

He had worked from home permanently since the children had been there and it had been successful. He needed the offices in Leeds, but the office manager was making an excellent job of overseeing business there and the company was doing better than ever. He knew that it would involve a drive to the office every week at some point, but the benefits of the schools in the village and the life that the children would lead there would make it worthwhile. And Beth would stay on.

He had a lot of sorting out to do, but he was convinced he had to start to make progress with Beth so he sent her some flowers, thanking her for all she had done.

She was startled to receive them: she didn't want or need his flowers or his thanks. What she had done had been for Martha and Harry: she had been prepared to go for weeks without being paid. True, he had paid her the missing wages as soon as he had been made aware, but that was irrelevant. She had never looked for his gratitude or rewards.

Chapter Thirty-Six

Tom Grace had no idea that Beth had any connection with The Willows or that living there again had been part of her rehabilitation. His only objective was to either transfer the existing tenancy to himself or negotiate a new one to secure her continuing care of the children. He asked her if she knew who the letting agents were but all she could suggest was that he try Linnell's, the agency in the village.

He decided to give them a try and found The Willows was on Linnell's books. His call presented the Linnell partners with an immediate solution to their problem without incurring any effort or expense and they were only too delighted to negotiate with him.

Beth had been quite right. The rent had not

been paid since the storm broke so the terms of the lease were broken and there were only seven weeks remaining on it. To further complicate their situation, they had not been able to contact Tess. The lease agreement was in Oliver Hargreaves' name and clearly, he was out of contact, so she was their only hope. They had Tess's number, but she had not answered, despite all their messages.

Tom offered them an ideal answer as a new tenant because he had sufficient liquidity to take over the weighty rental, and they deemed themselves free to settle things with him.

He was quite specific in his requests. He wanted the house emptied of all belongings, with the exception of the nanny and the children's things. As far as he was concerned, the Hargreaves things should be put into store. In addition, he wanted the house professionally cleaned and all the locks changed.

If he was to make a home in The Willows, he wanted it to be his home in both law and substance. His terms were no different to what any new tenant would expect. The partners at Linnell's were glad to have the matter resolved so swiftly and were able to advise him that the house would be ready for occupation within eight weeks.

He wanted to check that Beth would be staying

on if they were to move back to the village before he actually signed the lease. She was relieved to hear his news as it solved her dilemma and she agreed readily.

She was getting anxious about Matthew. Every time she saw him he looked thinner and more tired and she would be glad to be back nearer to him to keep a closer eye on him. He was pleased with the development at the centre, but the needs there were expanding too quickly to find sufficient volunteers, so the extra tasks increasingly fell on him.

He still had his one able assistant: Stefan, the silent giant of a young man who toiled ceaselessly without complaint. He was long-term unemployed because of his mental health conditions and he was regularly homeless. The centre had become his salvation.

Matthew turned a blind eye to him sleeping over in the centre occasionally whilst he found new accommodation because he relied on him so heavily. He had also taken the precaution of making sure Stefan was CRB checked and he was in regular contact with his social worker.

He was satisfied that whilst ever Stefan was taking his anti-psychotic drugs he represented no threat. He was extremely grateful for his support, knowing he could not manage without him. Stefan, though largely silent, was totally reliable and his menacing stature imbued the place with a sense of order. Would-be-trouble makers were put off trying anything because of his looming presence. None of them would have been prepared to take on this sinister-looking individual with the bear-like stature.

Matthew used to watch him with appreciation as he worked tirelessly each day. There was nothing he would not tackle at the centre, even the most unsavoury tasks, such as unblocking drains and toilets. Whatever he did, he did to perfection in his mechanical, expressionless way.

There was now a laundry with two industrial-sized washing machines and two large driers in constant operation. The shower rooms were also in constant use. Many of the clients lacked the facilities to keep themselves or their clothes clean and were glad of the facilities. An endless supply of donated towels had to be sourced and kept clean and Stefan took on their washing and drying each day.

There was a breakfast of cereal and tea every

morning and a late lunch of soup and bread. Matthew had got an agreement with a soup manufacturer and they supplied catering-size tins free of charge as they neared their sell-by dates. There were many consecutive days when the same flavour was served, but that drew few complaints. The bread was the remains of the unsold stock from the local bakery the previous day and could be white, brown, sliced, unsliced or any other type from their range. It was as fresh as most people would eat in their own homes and far better quality.

As soon as the tables were cleared from breakfast they were rearranged into groups. There was a basic literacy session and a basic numeracy session, and some tables were devoted to assisted form-filling. There were also two old computers linked to the internet for job-seeking and Matthew made sure that the parental controls available were fully utilised. He didn't want his clients using them to watch porn.

For those who wanted none of those there were a few daily newspapers and old magazines, provided by the local supermarket. There were also endless supplies of tea and coffee from the urns that were kept topped up all day.

Stefan thrived on routine and stability and the

daily rhythms of the centre suited him to perfection. He also idolised Matthew: he had never experienced genuine kindness and concern from anyone before and he would have done anything to please him. Stefan was Catholic by birth, so he transferred all his expectations of the Catholic priesthood on to Matthew and he did not approve of him having a lady friend.

When Matthew took Beth to visit again, she was stunned by the progress he had made. The food bank was still in operation five days a week, but all the other services had been built up very quickly.

She still wasn't confident about Stefan's suitability. She felt intimidated by his stature and silence. He had a menacing presence, and he seemed to resent her on sight, but she could see how much strain he took off Matthew's shoulders and, for that, she was grateful.

Matthew outlined his plans for an overnight shelter that he was planning to open within the next few months: an elderly parishioner had died and left his estate to the diocese and the proceeds were earmarked for the shelter.

"Isn't it too much too soon?" Beth asked.

There was silence.

"Please don't tell me you are taking that on, on top of all this?" she said.

It was difficult for him. He knew that there was a crying need for overnight shelter and, as winter approached, it was becoming more urgent to provide one. He knew he would be pushing himself too far, but everywhere he looked he saw need and so he stretched himself.

In his quiet, reflective moments he honestly admitted to himself that he did not know how he could sustain the demands on him. He was terrified that he might fail someone in desperate need and his prayers had been focused on that for some time.

He still prioritised prayers for others, but he needed help from somewhere because he knew he was dangerously close to his limits. He was also scared that his problems arose from hubris: the pride he took in trying to provide all the answers.

At least, for Matthew, there was good news because Beth was coming back to the village with the newly formed Grace family and there would be no more tiring return trips to Bradford.

Chapter Thirty-Seven

The move back to the village went smoothly, although the arrangements in the house changed considerably.

It was time, he said, for the children to have their own rooms. He also wanted his children living in the main house and being part of everything. He did not want them holed up on that top floor out of his way, so he took that over for his business.

He established his office up there just as he had had in his own home, which was now let through an agency. He installed his drawing board, tech equipment and phone lines in the nursery play-room. He took over what had been Beth's bedroom for himself and used the children's room for storage. Piles of files had built up since he opened the business and he sometimes needed to access them.

"Are we going to live in the real house?" Martha asked when he told them his plans on their arrival.

"Of course you are," he told her. "And you can choose your own rooms, only you can't have mummy's. That's for Beth."

Beth started at that. The last thing she wanted was Tess's room. She wasn't staging a takeover and she really didn't need the cavernous room and its extensive dressing room and en-suite.

"I thought I'd take the room you used to use," she said. "It suits me better." It was actually her old bedroom and she longed to be back in there. The Willows was good for her and would help mend the harm done by the stay in Bradford.

"I want you to realise how much we appreciate you. You must have the master. It's stupid to leave it standing empty."

"If Beth doesn't want it, can I have it?" Martha asked, in total innocence.

"No. You and Harry are to have rooms that are fair," Tom said. "You wouldn't like it if Harry had the great big room and you didn't."

"I just want a Harry room," Harry observed.

"And you shall have one," Beth said. "But I am

not taking over your mummy's old room. Anyway, it would be nice for grandma and grandad to feel they have a special room here now that they have got to know you."

Tom sighed. He conceded she had a point. In fact, she had an excellent point.

He had had to come clean with his parents and they were shattered when they learnt what he had done. They were hurt by what he had kept secret from them and shocked by what had happened since.

They took time to analyse and process it all and stepped back from him whilst they came to terms with it. At first it seemed incestuous and sickening as they had tried their utmost for so many years to treat Tom and Tess as brother and sister. They also disliked the hurt Tess had heaped on them by depriving them of all contact with the children and wondered if it was too late to bond.

They loved Tom beyond words, but they felt betrayed. It was as if both their children had stabbed them in the back, and they knew they did not deserve it.

Eventually they began to understand the torture he had put himself through, first of all in giving in to help Tess, and then having to keep it a secret from them. Finally, they agreed to meet Martha and Harry and from that moment all their issues with Tom faded away.

Meeting the two children made them immediately understand why he had had to keep seeing them in secret. If they were honest, knowing Tess as they did, they could see why he had hovered over them both since Harry's birth. They accepted he had been impelled to take over their parenting when Tess deserted them and why he had moved to West Stanton to give them the best possible life.

In one way he admired Beth for not taking advantage of the situation and seeing the need for his parents to feel they had a base in his home. He wanted them to bond with Martha and Harry, but he was getting nowhere with his attempts to foster a closer relationship with her. He had decided on a very gentle approach, but she politely declined any scheme he came up with that put them alone together.

She was happy eating with him and the children in the kitchen but she wouldn't eat with him alone in the dining room once the children were in bed. She wouldn't join him in the orangery for a glass of wine at the end of the day, but she would happily sit with him and the children to watch TV before their bedtime. He knew she saw her position solely in terms of her role as their nanny and she had no wish to blur the boundaries with him. She resolutely avoided any opportunity he made to redefine them.

He was going to have to try another approach, but, as they settled back into the village, he had no idea what. He did notice that she seemed more relaxed, less nervy, now she was back in the village. She was taking the children out and about in the Corsa confidently now, whereas she had seemed terrified to venture out into Bradford.

She was certainly an enigma to him: there was clearly a lot he didn't know about her. Those scars played on his mind: he was sure the answers were connected with them. Above all, he accepted that he was no expert where women were concerned as his successes with them in the past had been very limited. He just had to keep trying.

Chapter Thirty-Eight

Tom Grace realised more and more how good things would be if only he could make Beth a permanent fixture in their lives. His attempts to draw her into spending time alone with him failed every time, though she was always totally pleasant in her refusals.

He saw more and more that she was above all an honest person, and the more he thought about it, the more it seemed that the only honourable way forward was to be open and direct. She had, after all, been totally on his side once he told her his story and there was no doubt that she loved the children.

He could hardly proclaim undying love for her: she would see through that immediately, although he was fond of her. He was still unsure about where she stood with the priest. He could not bring himself to think of him by any other name. To call him Matthew would make him a real person with feelings. Calling him the priest made it seem as if he operated on a different plane. A plane that kept him on a path of celibacy, though he realised his assumption was based on total ignorance. All this reasoning was irrational, but it helped because it made everything seem possible.

He didn't feel good about this. Matthew had been an ally who had stood by him through the storm and supported his fight for parenthood of the children in any way he could. He had tolerated having to share his time with Beth with Martha and Harry tagging along without complaint. It was also annoyingly clear that the children were fond of him.

However, in Tom's head, he had to be the priest. He had created a box for him in his mind and slotted him in it because it meant things were not complicated. Tom was aware in his lowest moments he was deluding himself and was also aware he was far from being honourable. He wanted to take the woman Matthew Thomas clearly loved and marry her as a solution to his long-term domestic issues.

This had been playing over in his mind for

weeks when he decided he would simply present Beth with the future as he saw it.

It was Thursday evening. She had put the children to bed and had come down with their washing. She had gone straight into the laundry to set the machine going. He followed her; a lump of anxiety lodged in his throat so large that it made his voice sound croaky when he spoke to her.

"Can you spare five minutes please, Beth?"

"I'll come through when I've got this sorted," she said, oblivious to the thunderbolt he was about to launch her way.

He went through to the kitchen and sat waiting and she came in and sat opposite him with a sigh. She was weary that day and was glad to take the weight from her legs.

"I want to talk to you because I'm anxious to secure the future for Martha and Harry," he said. "I'd like you to become a permanent part of their lives."

"I'd like that too," she said because she couldn't imagine her life without them. She had, of course, no idea what he had in mind.

"I really like you, Beth, and I think it would be fantastic if we got married and became a real family," he said.

Her stomach plummeted and her heart began to thump to the extent that she could hear blood pounding in her ears. She went white.

"I'm asking you to marry me," he said. He reached across the table for her hand, but she withdrew it abruptly.

She stood up and pushed her chair in with meticulous over-precision. It was totally stupid, but it was the only thing she could think of to do as she felt the panic rise.

As he watched her fastidiously positioning the chair he caught sight of her face. He could see there were tears running down her face and he couldn't comprehend why. Had he upset her? Was she hurt? Was she crying with relief? He simply didn't know.

"I'm going to my room," she said, finally abandoning her adjustments to the chair.

She went upstairs, threw herself on to the bed and curled up into a ball. She cried silently with rivers of tears pouring down her face. This was no time for her to think or reflect. The simple truth was she was in shock: emotional shock that was manifesting itself physically and she surrendered to it entirely.

Chapter Thirty-Nine

Tom Grace had unwittingly opened the flood gates that Beth had kept tightly shut since the day of the attack.

Now, curled up in her foetal ball, her mind was suddenly awash with all the things she had resolutely refused to face and discuss. She was frightened at the intensity of their impact as they flooded in. The physical, debilitating effects of the attack had been devastating but this was worse. Would she ever regain composure and control?

She could hardly keep up with the pace of thoughts crashing into her head like storm waves breaking on the shore. Marriage. Intimacy with Tom. She felt violently sick. It was not about Tom Grace: she would never have married him. It was about her life and what had been ripped from her for ever that night.

Wayne Jackson had robbed her of any prospect of marriage. She would be forever denied love and intimacy because of what he had unleashed upon her.

Did she even want to get married? What would any man want a marriage without intimacy for? Where did all of this leave Matthew? How could she live without him? How long would he tolerate the distance she kept between them? She loved him yet she had never even been able to let him kiss her.

If that was how she felt about a simple kiss, how would she ever hold a child of her own? That last thought was the most horrific of them all. Had that man taken away all her hopes of motherhood? She now saw Martha and Harry had been her placebo for that well-suppressed ache. Did she have to keep working as a nanny to secure a future that involved children? Tom Grace had certainly made it impossible for her to remain in his children's lives now: she could not imagine ever facing him again.

The anger her doctors had expected her to show now surfaced, more powerfully than she could handle, and waves of torment kept repeating themselves and crashing through her brain. She had proved them all wrong up until that moment, but now her obstinate denial wasn't working. Her defences were breached and couldn't keep the turmoil out any longer.

All he, that wicked monster, had to do was to say sorry and his guilt would be gone for ever. What did she have to do to get rid of this tumult that had unleashed itself? Where would the strength come from to get it back under control? Where was her redemption?

Tom Grace was totally unaware of the cause of the storm that had struck Beth down. She had played her part as the shy, resourceful, sensible, reliable nanny so well that he had imagined her rational mind would have appreciated his honest offer of marriage and considered it logically.

He understood that she was incredibly distressed, beyond anything he could have imagined. That night he had tapped on her door and peeped in. No sound had come from within, but he saw her curled up, as if in agony, and he wondered what harm he had done. Memories of her scarring drifted into his mind. He remembered her terror at the prospect of settling in Bradford. He suddenly had the sickening feeling that he had, in total innocence, awoken her inner demons. He felt distraught but completely helpless and spent a restless night contemplating a way forward.

In the morning he stirred early and again tapped on her door and peeped inside. It was as if she had never moved a muscle and he realised he had to do something. She was still crying but made no sound.

"I'll look after the children today," he said. "You just do what you need to. I'll bring you a cup of coffee in a minute."

He went straight down and called the priest. "Can you come round right away?" he asked. "I'll explain when I see you."

He made the coffee and delivered it to her bedside table and he saw her face clearly for the first time. Her eyes were red and swollen and her skin had a pallor he had never seen on any living person, not even when he'd found her unresponsive with pneumonia. He was scared.

Matthew was there within twenty-five minutes. The children were still asleep and so Tom had the opportunity to explain what had happened. He put aside his shame and awkwardness because he knew the priest needed the truth. It was the most excruciating conversation he had ever had.

Matthew listened gravely, aware of exactly what

could have erupted for Beth and equally aware that no fault could be levelled at Tom Grace for that. He was furious that the man had had the audacity to offer to marry Beth to secure a surrogate mother for his children but his primary focus was Beth and so he put that aside and went upstairs.

His panic rose at the sight of her and he went straight to the bed to sit beside her. She uncurled herself slightly, sat up and moved in close to his waiting arms. This was not a lovers' moment. It was like a much-loved parent giving comfort to a frightened child and it brought a sense of calm to them both. They did not speak, they just held on to each other and she buried her head deep into his shoulder.

He had always known that the time would come when she would eventually have to face her demons, and he prayed he was equal to the task of bringing her through it unscathed. The strains and pressures of running the centre faded into the background now and he dropped a kiss on the top of her head, so gentle that she didn't even notice.

Chapter Forty

Eventually Matthew formed a plan that he managed to start to put it in place whilst he sat with Beth. He texted a friend who owned a cabin in a parkland retreat and arranged to borrow it for a few days.

He texted his centre volunteers and arranged a patchwork of cover for the next few days and finally contacted Stefan to ask him to monitor the place throughout his absence.

He told her of his plan and asked her to set about getting her things together. His request penetrated her awareness and she wearily got up and, as if in a trance, mechanically opened drawers and assembled a pile of items. He found a bag for her to put them in, glad that her packing meant she had given her approval to his plan.

He explained he would go and tell Tom, as succinctly as possible, what had happened to trigger her meltdown. She offered no objection so he went downstairs.

Tom was staggered when he heard why his proposal had provoked her reaction and he was filled with even more regret and remorse.

Matthew told him that he intended to get Beth away somewhere quiet where they could walk and talk and, he hoped, restore her balance. Tom was a practical man; he could do nothing to put right the harm he had done but he could put some food together for them. He raided the larder that Beth kept well-stocked and gathered up some provisions for them. He also offered to pack a bag to tide Matthew over for a couple of days so that they wouldn't have to detour into town to collect his things.

Matthew would not usually have considered borrowing someone else's things but it made perfect sense that day to get away as soon as possible. Tom offered to apologise to Beth but, on reflection, they both decided that it was too soon for that. Matthew promised he would pass the message on when the time was right.

They embarked on a silent journey. It wasn't an uncomfortable silence. Matthew realised Beth had nothing to say and it did not bother him. Beth's overworked brain had worn itself out and the pills she had taken took her back to the state of blankness that had once characterised her existence. It was not where she wished to be, but it was preferable to coping with the tornado that had whirled through her thoughts after Tom's proposal. She knew she couldn't allow herself to return to dependency but she needed some peace.

Matthew was worried that she could have had a major relapse because she was so detached and remote, even though he knew she was sedated. It had taken so long for her to forge a meaningful life and now he was afraid of all that progress being lost. He didn't have any answers, but he hoped a complete break and a change of scenery would trigger a recovery.

He collected the keys from the reception building and drove along the narrow, tree-shaded path to the cabin. It was in a beautiful setting, surrounded by pine trees. The wooden cabin, with its railed veranda and swing seat, looked welcoming and safe. He breathed a sigh of relief and was glad to see Beth lean forward to take in the sight.

It was magical inside too. It was small, but incredibly cosy with its logged walls, wooden floors and wonderfully welcoming and opulent soft furnishings. There were two bedrooms, a twin and a double. They were simply but adequately furnished, and the sumptuous fabrics again elevated the rooms to a feel of luxurious restfulness and calm.

Beth helped Matthew unload the car in a silent, mechanical way. They stowed their bags in the bedrooms. Beth opted for the twin for no particular reason: the room she was to use wasn't important.

Matthew unpacked the food.

"Hope you like bread," he said cheerily as he saw what Tom Grace had provided. To be fair, he had gathered together a survival kit with all the essentials for tea and coffee, as well as an assortment of tins and refrigerated items. "Let's get something to eat and then go for a walk. I need to stretch my legs after that drive. Will you work out how to put the kettle on?"

She managed to make coffee for them in her

detached state as he assembled some cheese sandwiches. He watched her automated response with a sadness deep in his heart but took comfort that she was responding to his attempts to restore normality. He knew she was unlikely to want the hunky sandwich he made for her, but he was hungry and at least these activities kept her moving and filled the silent spaces.

It was a fine day for late autumn and, after eating, he chivvied her out for a walk. The sun was strong and the afternoon was warm, though he was sure it would go chilly after sunset. They toured the veranda that surrounded the house and found a hot tub screened by rose-clad trellis at the back. The roses were hanging on defiantly to their last display before the frosts came. It would have been perfect to relax in the tub in normal times but it was too much for the day they were struggling through.

The sun encouraged what birds still remained to sing at full volume and the dry weather made the walk easy underfoot. They were treading on a depth of freshly fallen pine needles and their steps felt cushioned and perfumed. As they walked he was surprised to feel her slip her arm into his and he squeezed it to bid it welcome.

They found some tree stumps to sit on and survey the scenery. They could hear running water and suspected a waterfall was somewhere near.

"Thank you," Beth said, finding her voice for the first time. "This is just what I needed."

He turned slightly to see her better and the blankness that had enveloped her face was receding as she took in, and responded to, their surroundings. He could see she was concentrating on her breathing, but in a way that seemed appreciative of the fresh air.

They walked on in the direction of the sound of the water and eventually found the collection of rocks that caused the water to change its level. They watched its hypnotic small cascade of tumbling foam, breathing in the smell of damp pine needles. Subconsciously, they absorbed the water's energy that echoed in the sounds around them.

Again, she slipped her arm through his. It was too soon for her to try to talk but it was time for the shockwave of anguish to start to subside and she sighed heavily, as if physically expelling it from her body.

Matthew was so attuned to the woman he loved that he could detect and interpret these signs and, for the first time, the heaviness inside his chest light-ened slightly. Perhaps they had found a way through the nightmare that had finally overwhelmed her after it had held her in its thrall for so long.

Chapter Forty-One

Dinner was beans on toast, provided by Tom Grace's hasty food packing. It was surprising how appetising the smell of toast under the grill seemed in the confines of the cabin. Matthew had found some bottles of Pinot in the fridge and declared that he would replace what they used because their meal that night demanded wine.

He only poured her a tiny amount, aware of the pills she had taken earlier. He felt relief as he watched Beth begin to eat because she hadn't touched a thing all day. Her chunky cheese sandwich had ended up in the bin. She started halfheartedly by cutting a tiny triangle off the corner and chewing it for an age, but then she straightened up in her seat and cut with more speed and deliberation and ate with relish.

"I didn't know I was so hungry," she observed, speaking as if she had never lapsed into her long silence, "and I didn't know beans on toast could taste this good."

Matthew smiled and took a welcome sip of wine. Thank the Lord for Heinz he thought to himself, amazed at the impact of such a simple meal.

"Are there any beans left?" she asked as she finished the last forkful.

"Plenty. I'll join you," he said, putting two more slices of bread under the grill and giving the beans a stir. "They always taste better when the sauce has thickened up a bit."

She watched him as he busied himself and she was suddenly overwhelmed with love for this kind and patient man. He had come to her rescue once again. It came as a shock to her, but she was responding not just to that day, but to the months of care he had lavished on her. She had spent so long holding back her fears and anger she had forgotten what it was like to experience something so good totally engulfing her. She had loved him before, but she had never felt like this.

She topped up her glass of wine, knowing she was back in charge of her senses, and said nothing of her sudden surge of realisation as he came back with replenished plates.

"Thank you," she said, and set about the extra slice, at the same time looking at him with what felt like fresh eyes.

He had such a good, open face. It was the sort of face that made people trust him immediately. His eyes were kind. They were a browny-green colour, although he said they were hazel. Despite their tiredness that day they lit up when he smiled at her. The skin at the sides wrinkled into its well-established smile-lines.

His brown hair was starting to show the first traces of grey, but it suited him. He had it cut regularly in a desperate attempt to keep his wayward curls under tight control. He had a habit of running his fingers through them when he was concentrating which made him look tousled and boyish.

She took in these details and it was as if she was seeing him for the first time, and she started to feel warm inside: the sort of feeling that had eluded her for so long. Could it possibly be real love, rather than the affectionate love she had previously had for him, or was it the wine? She checked her glass; she had only taken a sip so far.

The cabin had a dish washer, so they loaded their dishes, wiped round and retired to the veranda with one of the voluminous throws that adorned the couches. They settled into the swing seat and she snuggled close to him, as she used to do when they watched films together.

It was chilly outside, the sky was cloudless, and the moon and stars were adding splendour to a velvet sky.

It was time to talk.

"I'm not sure what's happened," Beth said, "but since our walk I feel as if a weight that I've been carrying for so long has gone."

She looked skywards, "Look at all that. I haven't looked at the sky for ages. How can I keep letting him rob me of all this?" The stars were particularly bright that evening and every detail of the moon that could ever be discerned by the human eye was clearly visible.

Her response to the change in environment had been transformational and it was like a spiritual awakening. It was as if her eyes were once again receiving colour images of beauty from the world after months of viewing it only in shades of grey.

"Wayne Jackson," she said deliberately. "Wayne Jackson." She had never said his name aloud before. She found that nothing actually happened when she said it. It had no power over her or her surroundings.

She threw back her head and shouted "Wayne Jackson" at the top of her voice and no echo returned him to her.

This had been a test. If she said his name and nothing happened, then it meant he wasn't all-powerful and ever-present.

"He's not here." There was triumph in her voice. "There's just you and me and he can't stop me seeing the stars and enjoying being close to you."

She snuggled into Matthew more closely, becoming aware of what remained of the smell of the soap from that morning, and the roughness of the stubble developing on his unshaven face. Her words were a statement of the obvious, but he understood exactly what she meant, and he prayed that the suffocating hold that man had had on her was finally exorcised.

"I've enjoyed working with the children and seeing them develop, but it was always as if he was round the next corner or behind every door, just waiting to pounce. That made me just go through the motions of real life. It was getting easier to function, but I wasn't living, I was just looking after them and repressing any thought that could bring that night back into my head. I was scared that if I didn't keep busy with them, I'd lose my purpose and the doors to my memory would burst open. That's why I wouldn't talk about it in the hospital and I haven't talked since."

He could see how tenuous her hold on day-to-day life had been more clearly in that moment than he had ever been aware of, even though she had been his primary concern for so long. It humbled him that she had dissembled so successfully and he had not recognised her subterfuge.

She tried to explain the hurricane that had ripped through her when Tom asked her to marry him, and it all went back to that night. She had known, subconsciously, that she was using Harry and Martha as surrogates for the children she knew would never have. Wayne Jackson had made her so scared of human touch that she had accepted that she could never experience motherhood. Tom Grace's proposal brought the thought of intimacy into her head and she had lost all reason as memories of the rape came back: real and brutal.

"So, what's changed everything?"

"This," she moved her arm expressively to envelop the cabin, the trees, the sky and the heavens. "And this afternoon. And the smell of those beans on toast and the pine needles. And you. Everything's been here all along and I stopped seeing it."

Matthew was so glad they had made this trip together, although it had seemed at first that he was just trying to get her away from her despair. Now she'd broken through the nightmare that had taken her over for so long. It was as if he was hearing her real voice for the first time, and he liked what she had to say.

"And it was all because of you, always you, trying to help me find my way again," she said.

They sat in a peaceful silence looking at the stars, sipping their wine and feeling the warmth that was passing between them, physically and emotionally. It was a night neither of them would ever forget.

Chapter Forty-Two

Beth had found her fresh start, her new beginning, and as she lay in her bed, she went over the events of the past two days. What a journey it had been. In just over twenty-four hours she had gone from despair and agony to relief and the stirrings of love.

She could not sleep because she couldn't get thoughts of Matthew from her head. She could visualise him; she could remember that smell of soap, she could see his smile and as she did, she felt the gentle start of a thrilling surge of excitement in her stomach.

She lay on one side, turned to the other and stretched out on her back without being able to settle. A thought crept into her mind and it would not go away. She wanted to be beside him, she wanted to wrap herself round him and inhale his presence.

She slipped out of bed, crossed the hall and quietly crept into his room. Gently, she slipped into his bed and, as she did so, he stirred.

It took him some seconds to realise that the warmth beside him was Beth.

"You have to go," he muttered. "You can't be here."

He knew exactly what he wanted, and he knew how unthinkable it had always been between them. He had been forced to accept how abhorrent she found the idea of physical love and it was impossibly difficult for him with her lying by his side.

He was amazed to feel her move closer and put her arm around him, and he rolled over to face her, just able to make out her outline in the light cast from the hall lamp.

"I know you don't like to sleep alone," he said, "but I honestly can't share a bed with you."

He was starting to feel embarrassed in case she felt the effect she was having on him so he moved away slightly.

"I'm not scared tonight," she said," I just want to be with you."

"The trouble is, I can't be with you like this. It's just too much."

"It's just right," she said.

He could not believe his ears, and he was scared in case he was misinterpreting her words and in case any movement he made catapulted her back into her agony.

"I mean it," she said softly, reaching out and touching him.

"Beth," he said in almost a whisper, half-crazy with conflicting desire and common sense, "I haven't got anything with me."

The last thing he would have bought for that particular trip was a pack of condoms and he could hardly expect Tom Grace to have popped a pack into the bag of toiletries he'd sent along.

"It's OK," she replied, "I understand, but I really want this."

"And I want it too," he said, turning to face her again, heart pounding.

He loved her so much that this was a moment that he had not even let himself imagine. It was something he had thought was impossible, yet there she was, in his bed, in his arms and totally, totally willing to give herself to him. He kissed her tenderly and she sighed and relaxed in his arms.

This was a union where there was an instinctive trust between them, and a full understanding that the magic could disappear at any moment. That point did not arrive and they became lovers as if their bodies had been destined to become one as an inevitability.

These two uncertain and shy people come together for the first time with no knowledge of each other from the past. Every touch was new and every sensation was felt for the first time. Their experience was gentle, loving and utterly exquisite.

She closed her eyes as Matthew's ecstasy overcame him and she held him tight. They were finally fused together and nothing would keep them apart from then. It was a sealed contract between them, stronger than any certificate of marriage.

She had found love and she could give love, and he was the one man in the world with whom that would ever be possible, and she knew then she had no limits.

They curled together and slept peacefully and contentedly, both sighing as if, even in sleep, their bodies still remembered the pleasure they had shared.

They awoke in each other's arms and both knew that it had to begin again and that last night had been the start of something that would go on for ever.

"You look so beautiful this morning," he said as they lay sated and happy side by side.

"And you are wonderful," she replied. "So wonderful that I bet you even make morning coffee."

He smiled and rolled out of bed to make their drinks. He marvelled at how natural this all seemed, amazed that he was not scrabbling about to find a towel or some other cover, that her eyes followed him as if she were used to seeing him like that. When he returned with her coffee she was asleep, rolled into a little ball like a contented kitten and not in the desperate foetal position she had lain in for so many hours just the day before.

He marvelled at the aura of innocence that had surrounded her the previous night and earlier that morning after all she had been through, and, as he replayed moments in his mind that they had shared, he could not believe they had become lovers. He had never, at any time in his life, felt so complete as he did at that minute. He went away to shower and shave, luxuriating in the new feelings that were overtaking him. He knew he was tied to her for ever and he truly believed their union was as blessed as it would have been after a wedding ceremony.

Beth awoke to the smell of bacon cooking. It was drifting in from outside, where Matthew had lit the barbecue grill and was cooking the rashers that Tom Grace had put into their pack. He had a pan on the side ready to fry eggs and had set the little patio table with knives and forks.

Beth was no fan of cooked breakfasts but, that morning, the smell was so alluring that she dashed through the shower, pulled on her clothes and went out to join him. He had even made fresh coffee.

"You're a keeper," she said, sitting down, waiting for the food to arrive.

"So, my darling, are you!" he placed the plate before her.

It was smoked bacon. She had walked with Martha and Harry to fetch it from the farm shop the day Tom Grace had proposed to her. She usually wouldn't eat smoked bacon but that morning its smell was so irresistible that she ate with enthusiasm.

"We're lovers," she said, aware that she was

stating the obvious, but relishing the sound of the words.

"We're lovers," he repeated, smiling in the way he did only when he was alone with her. "For ever," he added.

"For ever," she echoed.

Both relaxed and slipped into their own thoughts as they sipped their coffee, and the silence between them was profound to them both in so many ways.

"What shall we do today?" Beth asked, breaking the silence as she put her cup on the table. "Shall we go for another walk?"

"Sounds perfect," he replied, "and we're going to talk."

"No more psycho-analysis for me," she said cheerfully.

"But maybe a little for me," he said.

She knew he was troubled about work and it felt so good to be able to be there for him now. She had seen the physical toll his work at the centre was wreaking on his body and she had suspected that it was also troubling his mind that the over-night shelter would stretch his resources to breaking point.

This was no morning for rushing. They lingered

over another cup of coffee, feeling the sun gain more heat as the morning wore on.

"I wish we could stay here for ever," he said.

She nodded in agreement.

That morning felt like the start of the best days of her life. The previous day she had shouted Wayne Jackson's name into the universe. Now she wanted to shout "I love Matthew Thomas" at the top of her voice and it felt wonderful.

Chapter Forty-Three

They retraced their walk from the previous day, intending to walk on further as they had more time. They re-discovered the seats that nature had thoughtfully provided and sat down close together.

"I've had a job offer," he said. The statement came out of the blue. He would have told her immediately it arrived, but the effects of Tom Grace's proposal on her had made him lay it aside and step in to help her.

"The church has an affiliated charity for the homeless and it's asked me to work for them as an adviser. It wants me to set up a network of day centres across the country based on the model I've just established. It's not just a church position, it's a developmental job for the charity."

He talked about the charity, a national organisation well-known to Beth for its network of charity shops and its commitment to maximising the amount of revenue passed on to the front-line work. She knew it was not going to be particularly well paid, but she also knew that would never be an issue.

She was pleased that his innovative approach had been recognised by such a respected organisation. She also knew how much it meant to him to be working at the centre, so she understood his dilemma about leaving it. But now was the time for her to listen, so she rested her head on his arm as he went on to speak his thoughts aloud.

"I'm so tired Beth," he said, and he sighed heavily. "Stefan's been a godsend, but he can only help with the practical stuff. The centre needs at least one dedicated social worker in addition to what I can do, and that is never going to happen. There isn't the money. The volunteers are great and keep the classes and the food bank running but it's the issues that come in. One day I'm going to miss something or not give someone enough support. I often don't have time to just sit down and listen and get the right things in place......I know there's a tragedy there just waiting...... I can't afford to take my eye off the ball for just a minute when I'm there. Sometimes, when I know I've not really got someone's problems sorted, I can't sleep in case something dreadful happens to them. To be honest, Beth, I needed this break as much as you. I'm scared that one day there will be someone's death or suicide on my conscience. I need to get back in control."

It all made perfect sense to Beth; she needed no further explanation. She knew how conscientious he was and how gravely he took his pastoral responsibilities. She had watched helplessly as he had become more exhausted and careworn.

"What shall I do? I don't want to let the centre down, but there's only so much I can do there. I can help more people through the charity. And I can work to make sure the new centres have adequate staff, as well as volunteers, as they set up. I've tried to do too much, instead of just doing what we can deliver properly. My pride has created this problem."

She was quiet for a second before saying "The problems you've created have happened because you've tried to meet all the need you see. That's not pride."

"I'd have regular working hours and we could

build a life together. You wouldn't be exposed to the sort of life I have been leading because, believe me, it's tough."

She nodded: she had seen, heard and even smelled the things he had been facing daily on her few visits to the centre.

"I'd have to do a fair bit of commuting, but it would all be within this county, so I could have a proper home life with you," he said.

He stood up. "Let's walk on," he said. "I need to think some more."

She felt honoured as they walked on. She was still central to the thinking of this good man and had been long before the events that had brought them there. Previously she had known she had to step in to make sure he was free to follow his conscience. Now it seemed to her that he simply had to make a choice for himself.

"I'm going to ask Tom Grace to find a replacement for me," she said. "I don't know if that helps you. I can't be the surrogate mother for Harry and Martha that he's looking for. They're not my children, though I wanted them to be, and that's hard to face. I need to step away. For God's sake, Tom was prepared to marry me to get me to stay on permanently. That's just not right. I can't stay on."

"So, you'd have no ties? We can choose what we want to do together?" He asked.

She nodded, and they linked arms and walked on.

"What would you do?" he asked.

"I think I'd go back to free-lance accountancy and work from home, wherever that is. I don't want to go back into the commercial world, but there are plenty of self-employed and retired people who need an accountant. It was starting to work before. Then I decided to help Tess out, and look where that decision has led me. Running a business from home could work."

"Which ever village that might be in," he added, knowing town and city life would never suit her again. "You do realise we need to live together?"

She squeezed his arm tightly, feeling yet another surge of happiness. This was so new and over-whelming to the woman who had simply been putting one foot before the other for such a long time.

"That's because we're lovers," she said with a smile, "and I never thought I'd ever be able to say that."

"I'm not sure being a lover is a very vicarly

thing to be," he observed, "but I like it. In fact, let's head back now. I switched the hot tub on before we left."

Beth answered in that totally innocent way she had of looking at things, "We didn't bring swimming things."

She giggled and blushed as she heard his reply.

"It's a bit late for us to worry about that."

And Beth knew then for sure that her scars would never be an obstacle between them despite all the time she had believed they had ruined her for ever.

Chapter Forty-Four

Tom Grace was amazed at the difference in Beth when she returned to West Stanton after three days away. She had left The Willows in an almost catatonic state and she returned glowing with a new inner energy that he had never suspected she possessed.

The children and the dog were overjoyed to see her, and they went with her as she carried her things up to her room, competing to tell her what they had done in her absence. Whilst they had missed her, they had not been bothered she was missing because Tom had kept them busy. That strengthened her resolve. She had built up their confidence and their independence and they would and could survive without her. She was not, as she

had sometimes allowed herself to think, indispens-
able to them.

The only problem she faced was that she had to
break the news of her decision to Tom, and she
resolved that it had to be that evening. There was
absolutely no point in putting it off as it would take
several weeks for him to advertise her position and
select a replacement.

He was not pleased to hear what she had to say,
and he cursed himself for the clumsy and heartless
way he'd tried to ensnare her into marriage to make
sure she stayed on permanently. He wondered how
he could have been so stupid to misjudge her
fragility and insecurity so badly. He kicked himself
that he'd been the one who had driven her away so
completely.

He tried to apologise and explain the good
intentions behind his offer but she stopped him.

"I know you were thinking of the children's
future and I'm glad that you wanted me to be a
permanent part of it," she said. "Let's leave it there.
And please, let's go on as if nothing has happened
until you can replace me."

"I doubt we'll come close to finding anyone as
good as you," he said, and he meant it, "but we will
do our best."

Things began to feel more relaxed and natural between them and she surprised him by accepting a glass of wine and going into the orangery with him that evening. They had just sat down in opposite chairs when there was a terrific hammering on the door.

"What the hell?" he said, moving quickly to stop the racket before it woke the children. The dog was barking and scratching at the kitchen door.

"Tess!" Beth heard him say, and within a second a wild-haired and wild-eyed Tess appeared in the room.

"You fucking bitch," she screamed at Beth. "You've ruined everything."

"Tess, keep your voice down, you'll wake the children," Tom warned.

Tess lurched at Beth as if she was going to pull her hair out and Beth dodged away, leaving Tom to take hold of Tess's flailing arms. She was totally uncoordinated, and he plonked her forcibly on the settee. A sequence developed in which she tried to stand and he pushed her down. It was clear then to Beth that she was in no physical danger from this drunken uncoordinated behaviour, although Tess's venom had disturbed her.

She caught sight of two frightened faces at the

door. "Come on," she said. "Mummy's not feeling very well," and she ushered them along the hall and back upstairs.

"Has Mummy come back for us?" Martha asked.

"I don't know sweetie, but I'll find out and tell you in the morning." By now she was at Harry's bedroom door, so she picked him up and popped him into his bed.

"I don't like Mummy," Harry said wretchedly, eyes wide open in fear. "She shouted."

Beth sat on Harry's bed and took Martha on her knee.

"We all get upset sometimes. Uncle Tom and I will help Mummy to feel better," she said reassuringly, though totally shaken up inside. "Now, everything's alright, so you just need to snuggle up and go to sleep."

"Will Mummy be here in the morning?" Martha asked.

"I honestly don't know," Beth admitted. "She might need to go and get some rest if she feels poorly."

She hugged Martha tight, "Let's get you back to bed so that I can go and look after Mummy."

Beth would have far rather stayed upstairs with

the two children, but she had to go downstairs to assist Tom. Her resolve surprised her but confirmed that she was getting her head straight at last and that, at least, was real progress.

By the time she had got Martha settled and had tried to answer her questions and reassure her Tom had managed to get Tess to sit still. She looked at Beth with hatred as she returned to the room.

"You fucking bitch. All you had to do was stay here and look after two children. Is that so much to ask? But you had to go running to Social Services, didn't you? I asked you to live in this lovely house, take care of two lovely children. That's all I wanted you to do. Too much for you, you had to call in the Social.'"

She was struggling to pronounce her words and was losing her cut glass way of speaking. "Get me a drink."

Beth did not move.

"I said get me a drink, a bloody drink," Tess repeated.

"You're having nothing else to drink," Tom said. "Not whilst you're here. And I was the one who contacted Social Services, not Beth."

Tess lurched as if to go to get herself a drink, but he put a restraining hand on her.

"Who told you to change the fucking locks?" she asked. "You had no right. Who said you could do that? This is my house. My house. Not dirty fucking Oliver's, and not yours, bitch."

"Enough," Oliver said, his voice like ice. "Enough!"

She looked at him and, even through the drink she could see the anger on his face, and, as she recognised the fury in his voice, she aborted her struggling attempts to fight against him get a drink. She flopped back on the cushions and closed her gaping mouth.

"Beth, could you get a glass of water for Tess please, and then make some black coffee?" Tom asked quietly. Turning to Tess he continued, "You are going to sit there, behave yourself and get some fluid inside you. We'll talk when you've calmed down and are making sense."

His words hit her like a bucket of cold water. Tom had had a hold over her since he had agreed to father her child and then keep it secret. That power was still working. It quietened her despite her drunkenness.

Beth returned with the water and then went to check on the children again. They were still in bed, curled up, but clearly straining their ears to make sure all was well downstairs. She spent a few minutes with each of them, assuring them everything was fine, and that Uncle Tom was looking after their mother.

Inwardly she grieved for the two of them. Their mother had returned after an absence of over three months and had not asked to see them or enquired after them. She was also so grateful that she had told Tom Grace of her decision to leave. This was all too much and she knew that she had to remove herself from the toxicity Tess had inside her, and this was possible now the children were settled with Tom. She was aware that her heart was pounding but her thoughts were clear and she felt strangely in control.

She returned with the black coffee and set it on the table by Tess's side. Tess looked at her with hatred and eyed the coffee as if it were poison.

"I want you to listen to me, Tess," Tom said slowly and deliberately. "This is my house now. Fact. I have custody of the children. Fact. You walked out months ago and have not even made a phone call in all that time to check on your own children. Fact."

It was as if three bullets had hit her.

"It's my house, they're my children and I've

been in hiding," she said in hopeless retaliation like a thwarted, petulant child.

Tom shook his head. "Wrong, wrong, wrong, Tess. I had to step in when Beth was left here with a horde of reporters laying siege, television crews on the street and no word from you. She turned to me. What do you think she should have done?"

"Waited. It was obvious I'd come back," again the childish petulance came through.

"You're going to drink your coffee, go to bed, sleep it off and we'll talk all this through in the morning."

Thank goodness I didn't take her bedroom, Beth thought to herself, imagining the tirade Tess would have launched at her if she'd taken over her space. She hoped Tess was in no condition to realise all her things were gone. She couldn't help but admire the way Tom had taken charge and was relieved she had not been there alone with the children. She wasn't keen on Tess being in the house overnight when she harboured such a grudge against her, even though she guessed Tess would flake out completely.

"In fact," Tom went on, "we'll take your coffee upstairs and get you to bed now. Come on then."

She stood up, head hanging down like a reprimanded child. She wasn't steady on her feet and so Tom half dragged her up to her old room. Beth followed behind carrying the coffee. She put it on the side table and left Tom to get Tess on to the bed whilst she closed the window drapes. She was glad to leave the room.

Beth needed to talk to Matthew. After she'd checked the children were asleep, she went to her room and called him. She told him briefly what had happened, and he said at once that he'd come over and spend the night.

After all that had happened, telling Tom Grace that Matthew was going to spend the night there was the least of her worries. She certainly wasn't going to ask his permission.

Chapter Forty-Five

It was a long night as they lay side by side talking quietly. There was so much to say, so much to decide, but the fact that they had come so far together and survived so much meant that they were able to start making plans.

Matthew was amazed at how Beth had come through the whole Tess incident relatively unscathed. Clearly she was hurt that, after all she had done for Tess, she had been on the receiving end of so much hatred, but she had not relapsed. She was keen to leave this domestic nightmare behind her now that she knew the children had managed so well with Tom.

Matthew had been able to call the bishop earlier that day and had told him of his decision. The bishop had invited him to his office the following day to discuss things further, so they focussed on that.

"I'm taking the job," he told her, "so I'll be asking the bishop to support my decision. I talked to the charity today and I accepted their offer verbally. I just have to confirm in writing."

It was such a relief to Beth to hear that. He had reached his own decision and she knew that he was perfectly at ease with it. It wasn't like it was before when he was desperate to set up the centre but didn't want to leave her. This time it was quite clear that what he'd decided to do sat well with him.

"I've got a chance to set up centres across the county and then, if they go well, extend the model across the country. I can't say no to that."

Beth was so pleased to hear the certainty in his voice. She was glad that he would be moving away from his hands-on role, which she knew put him into danger on a daily basis with clients with drug problems and criminal pasts. She also knew the anxiety he was living with about the inadequacies of the care he was providing and was glad this could stop.

"Have you spoken to Stefan?" Beth asked,

always uneasy about this constant foreboding presence at the centre.

"No, but I will when I've spoken to the bishop and know what will be happening. He always needs certainty, so I didn't want to unnerve him until I could be specific."

He wasn't looking forward to telling Stefan about the forthcoming changes because he knew how much the man relied on routine and structure to survive. He intended ensuring that his successor would take Stefan under his wing and keep him feeling valued and safe.

"So, tomorrow, when all that's done, we can set about finding ourselves somewhere to live, and then you can start planning your business," he said. "Who knows? We could be living together in a few weeks."

"That all sounds perfect," she said. "I have told Tom I'll be leaving as soon as there's a replacement for me." She paused for a second, "I doubt we can afford to buy a place, but we should be able to find somewhere to rent."

"We'll go over our finances tomorrow night and see where we stand," he said. "I don't expect our wedding will cost too much."

"Did you say wedding?"

"Didn't I mention that we'll be getting married as soon as we can?"

She felt a surge of joy. "No, you didn't."

He pulled her to him gently and kissed her. "I feel as if we're married already, or at least, spiritually joined." That sounded so loving. "And now we're going to make love extremely quietly," he said, dropping his voice to the lowest whisper possible, "because, as you are aware, we're lovers."

She loved his unique sense of humour and she giggled in delight.

Chapter Forty-Six

Tom Grace asked Beth to take the children out as early as she could the next morning. He knew Tess would sleep in and he didn't want them coming face to face with her whilst she was so unpredictable. He also wanted to prevent Beth having to face another tirade. He was hoping she would be more reasonable after a night's sleep, though he anticipated she would be heavily hung over. He was outraged at what she had said the previous evening.

He didn't know how he would feel about her having any contact with the children in the future. He was totally sure that she wouldn't be spending another night at The Willows and she certainly wasn't going to see the children that day.

Matthew had left just after six that morning, so

they didn't see each other. Tom wasn't pleased he'd spent the night with Beth, but he could hardly complain after the abuse Tess had hurled at her.

Beth got the children up and dressed. They headed out immediately after breakfast to visit the farm park. They were going to feed the animals and then go into the soft play area.

Tom had outlined his thinking to her and she was in total agreement. The thought of the damage Tess could do to the children's sense of well-being in her current state of mind terrified them both and made them desperate to keep them apart.

Eventually Tess emerged, freshly showered, ashen faced but as feisty as ever.

Tom took the lead immediately. "This is my house now, Tess, and you're my guest, so you can't start making threats and demands. We can talk things through and start to see where we go from here, but I warn you, we will be doing things my way."

"What do you mean, my house? This is my home," she said.

She clearly had not absorbed the consequences of ignoring all the emails, phone messages and texts that had been sent over the last months. She had been in a bubble of her own and had glanced at her phone as missives arrived, read the headline superficially and pressed delete without reading further. She could not be bothered; she had been so wrapped up in her own situation.

She had initially fled to the home of her long-term lover and had been made welcome at first, when it looked like a temporary arrangement. The glamour of an affair with the beautiful wife of a junior minister had soon faded into the reality of living with the ever-demanding, never-satisfied wife of a disgraced politician who was being held on remand and awaiting trial.

Things had deteriorated to the extent that one day, on returning from the hair salon, she had found her belongings dumped in his porch and the door bolted to prevent her gaining entry.

She had had no choice but to decamp to a cheap travel hotel where she could afford the overnight rate. Her monthly allowance into her personal account had stopped as Oliver's parliamentary income had ceased, and she was getting short of money. There were no meals included in the rate and she was not good at looking after herself, so she had been existing on a diet of lattes and pastries. She bought bottles of cheap wine in the supermarket and had drank them in her room from the bathroom glass, whilst she watched the endless streamed movies on TV from the comfort of her bed.

This was the Tess who had decided that maybe she would be better off at home, with Beth to wait on her and so she had turned up, only to find her key didn't open the door and her brother was firmly in charge.

Tom knew nothing of what she had been doing and wasn't particularly interested. He did, however, have to bring her up to date on the state of things with regard to her home and her children.

She listened incredulously as Tom outlined what steps he had taken. It had not occurred to her that things could move so fast without her consent. Every time she had pressed the delete key she thought she was buying further delay.

"So, you've now got my home and my children? It was you who contacted Social Services?" she asked. Her memories of the previous evening were fudged. "Some fucking brother you turned out to be. And what the hell have you done with my stuff? And why are you living in my house with the locks changed?"

"Don't swear at me Tess, it's not necessary," he said calmly. "The lease expired whilst you were away and Oliver was in no position to renew so I took out a new lease so the children could stay in their own home. The letting agents have had your things put in store and you'll need to contact them to get them back."

"Thank you very bloody much," she said. "So where am I supposed to live? And how do I get my children back?"

He sighed. These were questions that he either couldn't answer or didn't want to answer. "Things are going to be very difficult for you, Tess, but I'm sure you'll be able to sort things out."

"You're damned right. I'll get in touch with Oliver's parents. I'm sure their lawyers will put you in your place."

"I wouldn't bank on that. When Social Services contacted them about the children and told them my intentions, they found out that they weren't Oliver's biological children so they withdrew all interest and severed all contact. Whether they'd help you, I don't know, but they've no interest in the children now."

"You bastard," she said. "This was your plan right from the start when you offered to help."

"I've told you, don't swear," he said quietly, "and please remember I didn't offer, you wore me down with your pleas for help. It wasn't something I wanted to do."

She put her head in her hands, not knowing what she was going to do. She knew she'd not helped her chances of gaining Tom's assistance by the way she had handled things, and her old cunning returned. She replaced the fury on her face with a look of total vulnerability and helplessness.

"I'm sorry, Tom," she said, and wiped the corners of her eyes with her manicured fingers. "This has all come as such a terrible shock."

He looked at her in disgust and hardened himself against her tactics.

"It's Beth you should be apologising to," he said. "You came in here blaming her for everything and trying to attack her."

"I didn't know then what she'd been through," she said. "I'm so sorry. I know now she did her best," she said. "Not like my conniving brother." She was instantly annoyed with herself for letting her mask slip. "So, what do I do now? Get my stuff and move back in?"

"That's the last thing you're going to do," Tom said. "You are going to have to get yourself sorted, get yourself some money from somewhere, find yourself somewhere to live and pull yourself together. You won't be seeing the children until all that's done."

"I'm their mother," she protested.

"And I'm their father and I get to tell you how things will be."

She looked at him in total astonishment.

He remained cold and decisive. "Shall I call you a taxi? Don't worry, I'll pay."

The truth was she had no idea where she could go. Her bank account was almost empty. Whatever she did in the short term had to go on her platinum card and she'd worry about how to pay that off when she was absolutely forced to. She was thankful she'd not gone on the spending spree she'd thought she deserved to cheer herself up the previous week when her lover had evicted her.

A thought suddenly struck her that gave her hope. Her story could be worth something. She would contact some press agents and see what she could work out. She would definitely be keeping that to herself.

Tom called a taxi. Their meeting was over and all that was left was silence and broken bonds. Tess left and had never once enquired about her children.

Chapter Forty-Seven

Matthew met with his bishop and they agreed the arrangements for him to leave the centre. The bishop could see the move was good for all parties. He knew how important it was for the church to be seen to be looking after the most vulnerable, as well as preaching about it. This opportunity for Matthew moved their agenda forward more quickly than he could have ever hoped.

He had someone in mind to come in to take over and he said that he would speak to him formally now and get back to Matthew with proposals for a handover. He thought they would need at least two weeks of shared responsibility as a bridging period.

He did not mention that he had secured the funding to hire an extra person to join Matthew at the centre. He would still go ahead with that appointment when the money came through. For now, he would just find a replacement. There was no point dumping the fact that help had been so close for the conscientious priest.

After the meeting Matthew took Beth shopping. They went to the antique shops in the lanes of the nearby town to choose rings. It was all a matter of budget, despite the intensity of their relationship right then. Second-hand was the best option and Matthew wore his dog collar in an unashamed attempt to secure the best deal.

They chose a tiny Victorian ring with rubies and diamonds in a neat row. It was so small it had been in stock for such a long time that they were able to strike a very favourable deal.

He opted for a plain signet ring from the same shop, which he chose to have engraved with their initials intertwined. They also commissioned the engraving of "For all eternity" inside both rings.

They toured letting agencies to investigate possible homes and found a modest, furnished little house in the next village that had been built at the turn of the last century. It had been refurbished but still maintained its homely charm and stood at the end of a lane that led up to the local church. They viewed it during bell practice and the sound of the bells confirmed it was the place for them.

The village was small but was well-served with a post office, a grocery shop, a health centre, library and cafe bistro. They signed the agreements and paid the deposit without hesitation. It was eminently suitable for Beth's peace of mind and as a haven for them both.

They decided to leave their wedding until after they had settled in their home and Matthew was established in his new post. It was such a whirlwind they both felt that the wedding would be too much to organise with all the changes they had to face, and they felt joined in a way a marriage license wasn't going to strengthen.

Tom Grace had already arranged interviews to appoint Beth's replacement and all that was left to do was for Matthew to let Stefan know what was going on. He owed that to his tireless volunteer because he had made it possible to develop the centre the way they had. It was not a conversation that he was looking forward to. Although he held

Stefan in the highest regard, conversations with him were always difficult because of his predisposition for silence.

He made them both a cup of coffee one day when the centre was particularly quiet and sat down with him to explain. Stefan listened, those dead eyes of his betraying no reaction.

"You are leaving mother church?" was his only question.

"No," Matthew reassured him. "I could never do that, but I won't be at this church." He indicated the church down the street with his arm. "It will be the new manager's church though." Stefan's frown deepened.

"You are marrying your woman?"

'I will do one day," Matthew said. The silence from Stefan seemed to intensify.

"Stefan, this centre needs you. You are so important to everyone and I am sure you will like the new manager."

"I like you," Stefan said slowly and deliberately. "Only you. You are my priest."

They finished their coffee in silence and then both got on with their tasks. Matthew was still uneasy and telephoned Stefan's social worker about the forthcoming changes. Both knew how much Stefan's mental issues made him resistant to change so she said she would visit him and make sure he saw his consultant. She assured Matthew there was no more he could do but he wished there was.

He was not reassured, and he became increasingly anxious as the days went by. Stefan was as efficient as usual, but he was totally unresponsive to Matthew and he began talking to himself, but not in English. When the new manager arrived, he ignored him with undisguised bad feeling. He was talking to himself much more loudly as he went about his jobs.

Neither priest had a clue what he was saying, but he sounded angry and they were concerned. The social worker had promised to visit that week but there had been no sign of her, and a phone call revealed she was on sick leave.

Stefan was pointedly ignoring all of Matthew's attempts to engage with him.

Matthew talked this over with Beth and she was not happy at the deterioration in Stefan's grasp on normality. She begged him to be careful and was even more concerned to hear that Stefan was totally blanking his replacement.

As her period of notice dawned she showed the prospective nannies round the house, explained the routines and offered feedback to Tom Grace when he had interviewed them. Eventually a choice was made and a friendly woman in her early thirties with a sunny, practical disposition and excellent references was chosen. Her name was Julia and the children seemed to like her. They agreed a shared hand-over week and Beth began to gather her things together in readiness for her move.

Matthew stayed overnight more and more. Their attachment was becoming so strong that neither could bear to be without the other for any length of time. He had already packed up his belongings and was itching to move forward. He was taking two weeks' break before moving on to his new position and they planned to spend their time making their rented house into a home and assembling all the things they found they needed.

The children had been told that Beth was going to marry Matthew and that was why she was going to leave and live in the new house. They were told that Julia would be coming to look after them. They were happy because Beth had promised to visit them and take them to the park just as she always did. Martha asked if she could be Beth's bridesmaid, and Beth said she would have to ask Matthew.

"Well," Martha had said, "I'm his favourite girl, so I'm sure he will say yes."

Chapter Forty-Eight

Beth and Matthew moved steadily towards their new life. The rings were ready for collection and he picked them up before heading to the centre for his last day. He planned to take Beth out for a meal that evening so that they could exchange their rings in a romantic, candle-lit setting.

He was startled by Stefan's unkempt appearance that day. He was wearing the previous day's shirt and it bore the signs of the tomato soup he had served that lunchtime. He had not shaved and his hair, usually gelled and slicked back, was hanging lankly around his face in greasy strands.

He did not respond to Matthew or James, the new manager. He carried out his duties, but he was talking to himself even more loudly than usual, and it was as if he were carrying out a conversation with someone. It started to sound more like an argument, and he was becoming angrier.

Matthew grew concerned and rang the social worker: he was starting to think Stefan needed urgent medical assistance. She was still unavailable and he hesitated, unsure what to do. He sought James' advice and together they decided to call the emergency services and ask for help. He made the call, watching Stefan through the office door.

By this time Stefan was rowing with his imaginary companions, his voice echoing through the centre. Many of the regulars assessed the situation and left. They were used to life on the streets and knew the signs when something was going to kick off. James went around the centre as discreetly as possible and asked their remaining clients to leave quietly.

Emergency services said they would send out an ambulance and would arrange for police back-up. James made sure the centre was empty apart from Stefan and Matthew, then went outside to wait for them to arrive. Matthew was finishing the phone call.

Stefan absorbed the evacuation of the daily clients and his animated conversation grew louder and angrier. He started to back away from an unknown and unseen assailant and his only word, at the top of his voice, from then on was "NO!" His hands clutched his head as if the pain in it was so bad it would explode, and he backed into the kitchen and slammed the door.

Matthew realised that the call had kept him in the office for too long and wished he had used his mobile. He decided that his safest option now Stefan was shut in the kitchen was to leave the building immediately and secure the door behind him, leaving the tortured man alone inside.

He tried to move silently and had just reached the porch when the kitchen door burst open. Stefan came tumbling through the door screaming and rushed towards the exit. He was possessed by the frantic need to get out of the building, away from the demons he sensed behind him. Matthew was in his way.

Stefan held a knife in his hand, and, as he lurched into the porch, he grabbed a handful of Matthew's jumper and shirt and pulled him round. He plunged the knife deep into Matthew's chest, pushed him roughly to the ground, hurled himself through the door and tumbled flailingly out into the street.

The police response team had just left their vehicle and they charged at him without hesitation, crashing him to the ground, pinning him down and disarming him.

Stefan was bundled into the police van, struggling to break free from them, and was driven away.

The paramedics rushed to Matthew and quickly transferred him into the waiting ambulance. They closed the doors. The waiting was unbearable. James had no idea how bad he was and what they were doing. It took an age before they were ready to move away. They started the engine and pulled away, lights flashing and sirens blaring.

James went to the office to find Matthew's phone and searched through the contacts. He made two calls. The first was to the bishop's office to let them know what had happened and the second to Beth. Then he secured the centre and drove to the emergency department.

Chapter Forty-Nine

James met Beth at the hospital entrance and led her to the relatives' room in the emergency department where Matthew was being treated. They were not allowed to go to him.

He explained what had happened and Beth listened with increasing horror as she learned the doctors were fighting to save his life. She was shaking as the story unfolded.

They were offered tea, but neither wanted it.

A policeman came in to update them about Stefan. The suspicion was that he had stopped taking his anti-psychotic medication and had suffered an episode so bad he was seeing people and believed they were giving him orders. He had been taken to a different hospital for treatment but was under arrest and under police guard.

All Beth wanted was to go to Matthew and she found she was straining to listen for footsteps, wanting someone to arrive with news. She lost count of the times footsteps drew close and then faded away but, at last, the footsteps stopped, and the door opened.

A dishevelled doctor came in, still wearing scrubs that bore clear evidence of blood stains. His face looked strained and both Beth and James leapt to their feet fearing the worst.

He motioned that they were to sit down and, as he took his seat, their fears grew. He introduced himself, but later, neither Beth nor James could recall his name.

"You need to be aware that Mr…sorry, the Reverend Thomas has suffered a major injury to his chest and has lost a lot of blood. The stab wound missed his heart but punctured his lung."

He said it was nothing short of a miracle that the paramedics had arrived just as the stabbing took place. Matthew had saved his own life by making that call for help. The paramedics had had to work hard in the ambulance to get him stabilised before they could move him to the emergency department.

"We've managed to get everything under control, and he will be moved to the ICU in a few minutes. When we've got him settled in there you will be able to visit him for a while but be aware that he is still very ill."

He looked at them both, "Do you have any questions?"

Both of them were absorbing what he'd just said and had not processed it sufficiently to ask questions. They shook their heads.

Beth had just managed to say thank you when he stood and said he had to get back and that a nurse would be in to take them to see him shortly. They watched him leave, feeling relieved but totally stunned.

It seemed an age before the nurse arrived. James excused himself and left: he had only known Matthew Thomas for a few days and felt he had no further role there. He said goodbye to Beth, having made sure there was nothing more he could do.

Going into the ICU was like re-entering a nightmare for Beth but her anxiety for Matthew was so strong that it drowned the upsurge of emotion that erupted within her. She heard the familiar beeping of machines, took in the intensity of the artificial daylight and the anonymity of the staff behind their white gowns and masks.

She was led to his bedside. He lay with his eyes closed, his face covered by an oxygen mask. There seemed to be pipes and tubes and wires coming from everywhere. They put a chair for her at the side of his bed.

"He had these in his pocket," the nurse said, and she held out two ring boxes in her gloved hand. "The police took his clothes for their forensic team,"

Beth took the boxes and managed a nod of thanks.

"I'll leave you with him," she said, "but I'm only over there at the desk."

Beth opened the boxes and saw their rings, all cleaned and gleaming. She gently took his hand and eased his signet ring in place. Tears poured down her face as she kissed the ring and kept it at her lips for a moment. He didn't stir.

"Hello my darling," she said. "I'm here now and I'm not going anywhere, and neither are you." She put her ring on and then held her hand towards him. "Look, it's official. We're wearing our rings. We can't be parted now."

She rested her forehead on the side of his bed

and closed her eyes. She wasn't ready to lose him, not after all they had been through, but she was so afraid. All she had suffered was nothing compared to what she was feeling then. If she could have changed places with him, she would.

Again, her thoughts were coming into her head so fast she couldn't keep pace with them and this time Matthew was unable to comfort her or support her. From deep within she remembered her breathing exercises. She raised her head from the bed and, eyes fixed on him, she concentrated on his face and her breathing.

In through the nose and out through the mouth. She made herself concentrate and repeat that pattern until she felt control returning.

She took his hand in hers once again and began to pray.

It was not a well-thought-out prayer. It was a stream of consciousness, random thoughts that tumbled from her confused state of awareness.

"Please, please let him live. Please let him live. I forgive Stefan and I forgive Wayne Jackson so please let him live."

The words kept tumbling out. All the things she had never believed herself capable of saying. She had to pray. She had to say these things.

The forgiveness of Wayne Jackson was of no significance. He belonged in the past. Matthew was her present and her future.

Stefan had loved Matthew. He had been out of his mind when he struck. He was safe now and that was what Matthew would want. Matthew was all that mattered now, so Stefan had to be forgiven.

Matthew must not, could not die, and his God could not let him. All her bitterness towards Wayne Jackson meant nothing. Stefan was ill and could carry no responsibility. She forgave them both because they no longer mattered. Matthew did.

He wouldn't die.

She wouldn't let him.

Redemption had come and her past was buried at last, but what she faced was even worse. She was praying for her future and that future had to include Matthew.

Six months later.

The sun was struggling to shine on the spring morning when the letter finally arrived from the hospital. It contained the date for the surgery to remove the scarring that had tormented Beth for so long. It also confirmed her appointment with the plastic surgeon to discuss the procedure.

She read it and passed it to Matthew, who frowned as he scanned the contents.

"Maybe next year," he said in an attempt to give his reaction a positive spin.

"Or longer," Beth replied. She smiled. "We have things to do before then."

He was pleased to see the delay had had no impact on her at all. He put the letter back in its envelope, "I'll call them for you on Monday to postpone."

She watched as he put the letter on the dresser. Once again she felt relief at the weight he was starting to regain and she noted the developing fulness in his face. He was looking more like his old self after his long recovery and he was easing back into his role as her protector and organiser.

"Time to go," he said, as he secured their rescue dog in the kitchen. He locked the door behind them and looked at her with undisguised excitement.

They walked the short distance to the church hand in hand. The bells were already ringing out their welcome and, with a brief kiss farewell, Matthew made his way to the rear vestry door.

Beth entered through the porch to the main door to be greeted by Josie and Marie. Marie had brought flowers: a pastel cascade of peonies and camelia with delicate ferns. Beth took them from her with gratitude. It was such a lovely gesture on what was to be a simple but significant day.

"Beth!" Harry's young voice called out in excitement; his little mouth now sufficiently developed to cope with her name. "You look beautiful."

"So do you," Beth replied, taking in his polished appearance.

"I've got the rings," Josie reassured her, patting her bag.

She started as she saw Laura standing by the side of the hymnals inside the main door.

"She's standing in for the verger, apparently," Marie whispered to her. "She just had to muscle in. Don't let her spoil things."

"She couldn't if she tried," Beth replied.

Laura approached her and then stopped in amazement. She had not seen her after Matthew's accident and she had heard nothing about her since.

"You're pregnant," she said, stating the obvious as, at six months, the bump was well-defined.

Beth beamed." Yes. Isn't it wonderful? "

Her baby, conceived before Matthew was stabbed, was her miracle: the child she had once thought she would never carry. No one could ever tarnish the joy she felt at her prospective motherhood. If Wayne Jackson and Stefan were nothing, Laura was less than nothing.

Beth could see Matthew was already in position, so she sent Marie and Josie, their witnesses, to their seats whilst she arranged her little wedding party.

Martha walked in front and Beth followed, holding Harry's hand.

The poignant little trio processed down the ancient aisle of the small country church. Each one of them stepped out confidently, fully assured that they were loved and cherished.

The bells rang triumphantly as Beth and Matthew emerged as husband and wife. The small group gathered together for the photographs that Tom Grace was to take. Beth noticed he had to let go of Julia's hand as he stepped forward.

She was pleased he had found what he wanted. She could see he was full of pride that day: his children had shone in their roles; both had loved the attention the day had brought them and were beaming.

"We need to go now," Matthew said apologetically after the photography was finished and the congratulations had been said.

"The dog might destroy the kitchen if we don't get back," Beth explained. "We've never left him before."

They made their way through the lychgate and, once they were on the street, their friends launched a shower of confetti.

They walked home to face the potential mayhem in their kitchen to the sound of bells and the shouted good wishes of their friends.

It had, they said, all been perfect.

Acknowledgments

Thanks to Michelle Howes, Joy Ward and Chris Garbett for their support and advice.

Special thanks to Emily Sowter and Clare Lewis for believing in this project and for their encouragement.

About the Author

S.D. Johnson is an emerging author of contemporary romantic fiction.

Her aim is to tell compelling stories and also to challenge the reader intellectually in the moral dilemmas that her tales unfold.

You can follow her on social media and also on her website: sdjohnsonwriter.simplesite.com

 twitter.com/sdjohnsonwriter

 instagram.com/sdjohnsonwriter

Also by S.D. Johnson

I Needed to Drink Tea With You

Scorpion Tales

My Dearest Dolly

Printed in Great Britain
by Amazon